The Cowboy's
Untamed Heart

The Cowboy's Untamed Heart

A Sweethearts of the Rodeo Romance

Jamie K. Schmidt

TULE
PUBLISHING

Prologue

J ACKSON BLEVINS DID not want to be in another damned meeting. It was too fine of a day to be stuck in his office, even if he had the perfect view of Shelby Miller's jugs poking out of her prissy suit.

When the Women's Professional Rodeo Circuit and the Men's Professional Rodeo Circuit had merged in order to stave off bankruptcy, they'd combined their programs and events into one business called the United Professional Rodeo Circuit of America or UPRC.

They were still hemorrhaging money despite all their cost-cutting and financial consultants.

"You've got one more season, maybe two at this rate," their accountant, Benny, said with a concerned shake of his head.

"I don't understand," Shelby said, her voice showing the Georgia accent that she tried to hide. "When we made this deal, it was supposed to save both companies, not tank them."

"There were a lot of hidden debts and costs." Benny shot Jackson a look.

So fucking what? What was the point in being the CEO

of a major company if you didn't have some expensive perks?

"We just need to get attendance up," Jackson said, faking a reassuring smile at Shelby. "And we're working on that. Benny is just being an alarmist."

"The insurance policies are killing us," Benny said. "The veterinarian fees for drug testing all the horses and bulls are one of your biggest money sinks."

"I'm on that," Jackson said. "I've spoken to our policy holders, and they've agreed to waive the mandatory testings as long as we narrow down the breeders and stock suppliers to just a few trusted vendors."

Shelby frowned. "We've established several relationships with various farms and breeders across the country. How are you going to choose?"

"The ones who have the animals that perform the best will get first shot at being our exclusive suppliers. We need butts in seats. We need drama and excitement."

"We need to keep a cap on our spending," she said tartly.

Jackson's hand itched to slap that smartass mouth of hers. But you couldn't do that anymore, more's the pity. "You take care of the human athletes. I'll take care of the animal ones. We'll get through this."

He didn't like that Shelby and Benny exchanged a look he couldn't interpret. Shelby stood up and sighed. "We should have a meeting after every rodeo this season to discuss what we can do more efficiently."

Blevins bit back a groan. *Great. More fucking meetings.* "Fine." That wasn't the F-word he wanted to use, but if it got that little bitch and the nerd out of his office, he'd play nice.

"I'll be in touch," Benny said.

After he and Shelby left, Jackson poured himself a large Scotch and made a few phone calls. He had a buddy who worked on a few reality shows. He'd know all the dirty tricks on how to get people tuning in next week—or in this case, coming out to the rodeo.

Opening up his desk drawer, he took out his special box that contained the magic powder that kept him financially afloat—and a nicer person in general. He took a deep snort of the line and smiled. Jackson was looking forward to having his livestock supplier who made frequent trips in and out of Mexico for him coming into town next week. It wouldn't just be bulls and horses they'd be bringing over the border, either.

Chapter One

Reba Keller

Paris, TX—South Side Fair

D R. REBA KELLER loved the smell of fresh hay. She loved working outdoors and she loved animals. People on the other hand, well…people sucked.

"I don't know why this has to be this way," Karen said, standing way too close to Reba and the horse she was examining.

Reba wasn't sure the woman's name was actually Karen, but the attitude fit. She felt a little bad for all the Karens out there who didn't deserve the internet moniker of being a privileged snot who only thought about themselves. But in Reba's experience, there were more Karens out there than not. Or at least, they made their presence known more than the people who just wanted to go about their day and do their job until they could go home to their cat, dog, or potbellied pig.

At one point, Reba had had all of the above in her tiny apartment. But then her downstairs neighbor—another Karen—had complained that the pig sounded like she was wearing tap-dancing shoes at three o'clock morning, and

Reba had been forced to find another home for her.

That was probably for the best, even though she missed Pig Bundy with all her heart, because Reba had given up her apartment a few months later after she had quit her job at Kilgore Veterinary Services.

Homeless and jobless, Reba had decided to take a break from the office life and got into her parents' Winnebago to join the entourage for her baby sister LeAnn's rodeo career. Her parents hadn't let Reba take her dog or cat with them on the road. So her pets had stayed at their home in Paris, Texas, with her oldest sister Loretta. Reba missed them fiercely, too, but at least she was comforted by the fact that Loretta spoiled them rotten.

Before the UPRC hired her to look after the rodeo animals, Reba had earned her keep by taking care of LeAnn's horse. Her small salary, though, had been contingent on LeAnn winning. Reba had supplemented her income doing freelance veterinarian jobs, which were more common than you would think on the traveling rodeo circuit. While she didn't get to stock a lot of supplies—there wasn't a lot of money for it or a lot of room in the RV—Reba was able to keep the cowboys and their horses satisfied with her doctoring skills.

"Why is this feed so expensive?" Karen asked, her voice strident and nasal.

"You'd need to ask the people who are selling it. I'm just the veterinarian. And if you think that's expensive, wait until you see my bill."

Karen's head reared back as if Reba had slapped her.

"My husband is a rodeo star," she said, with her hand

over her heart.

"Good for him. His horse has kidney problems. You need a feed with low protein. Grass hay is preferable."

"I thought the UPRC covered all medical expenses."

After a year of traveling all over the country with her sister, Reba had been offered a permanent position with the UPRC, the new rodeo organization that combined the men's and women's rodeo circuits into one corporation. She was still feeling out the particulars of the job. But one of the perks was she didn't have to deal with a lot of people. Today was an exception.

"No, ma'am, they don't."

"That's ridiculous."

"You can take it up with the powers that be." Reba glanced at her watch. "Now, if you'll excuse me, I've got to check on a bred heifer."

The heifer wasn't anywhere near close to delivering, but it gave her an excuse to go to the farm exhibits of the state fair, and away from the rodeo arena.

"I want to speak to your manager," Karen shrilled her species' war cry.

"Knock yourself out," Reba said, glad that she wasn't working out of a veterinarian's office anymore.

"I find you very rude," Karen said.

"I've heard that before," Reba said over her shoulder. And in this very town, as a matter of fact. Paris, Texas, her old stomping ground. Her parents still lived here.

Three years ago, when Reba had worked at Kilgore Veterinary Services, Karen could have been one of her clients. If the rodeo had come to town and her cowboy husband was wondering why his horse had been acting lethargic, Reba might have been the vet on call who checked out the ulcers on the horse's tongue.

Reba had been in charge of the large-animal exams at that time. Dr. Kilgore specialized in domestic pets like dogs and cats, and also in being a misogynistic jerk. He was a man-child in a white lab coat who threw temper tantrums as often as he threw pens and other objects. To say it was a toxic work environment would have been an understatement, but Reba had loved her clients—even if she hadn't liked their owners. Crammed into the tight office space, Reba would have had to sit on the other side of the counter and take Karen's bad attitude with a smile.

"Don't you walk away from me," Karen shouted after her.

Nope, Reba didn't miss her old job at all. She didn't miss the customers, nor the antiseptic smells and the industrial cleaner that burned her nose so badly, she couldn't imagine how the animals with their keener sense of smell could tolerate it.

What she did miss was her patients: pregnant kitty cats, taking porcupine quills out of hound dogs' snouts, delivering calves, vaccinating horses, and doing the other daily treatments that all types of small and large animals needed.

Reba certainly didn't miss her boss's fits when the jars weren't put back in the exact order he wanted them to be in. She might have understood it if he wanted them in alphabetical order or grouped by medicine type. But no, he had his own system. It didn't make sense to anybody but him. Once you learned it, you knew it, but it wasn't intuitive. And sometimes when you got busy, shit happened. Then the whole office suffered.

"How did you fucking graduate college?" Dr. Kilgore would rage. He was an equal-opportunity screamer. He'd yell at the receptionists, the vet techs, and even the other doctors in the practice. One by one they all left. Reba had stayed for the animals, not for him, but when he launched a jar against the wall and a piece of glass sliced at her face from the blast, she knew she had to get out.

He had been apologetic, but it had been too late. And after being given a generous termination bonus and the promise of a good recommendation, Reba decided not to take him to court or have him arrested. But the workplace violence that she had experienced made her very wary of working in close, confined spaces, especially with loud-mouthed doctors. That was why she liked working the UPRC rodeo events. It was mostly wide-open spaces.

Dr. Kilgore had always been second-guessing her, too. He was a micromanager, a control freak, and a narcissist, the trifecta of asshattery. It had taken Reba a long time to stop questioning her decisions. Sometimes, she still heard him in the back of her head when she was faced with a tough decision or a more complicated diagnosis.

Reba's phone rang just as she entered the barn where the heifer was waiting her turn at auction. Expecting it to be one of her sisters, Reba was surprised that it was Diane Brolin, the coordinating supervisor of the UPRC veterinarians, and her boss.

"That was quick," Reba said.

"Were you rude to Vanessa Sunderland?"

"Depends. Is Vanessa a twat?" She could almost picture Diane closing her eyes and shaking her head.

"Please don't use language like that."

"I didn't call her that to her face." And Reba thought she should be given a fucking medal for that.

"She's pretty steamed at you."

"She's got her panties in a wad because the renal feed is double the cost of the crap feed they've been giving Starshine."

"Starshine?"

"I didn't name the horse," Reba said, rubbing the head of the heifer as it came to greet her.

Diane let out a huge sigh. "I need you to apologize."

"I'm sorry," Reba droned.

"To Vanessa, not to me."

"I don't have time for this shit." Reba didn't mind apologizing when she did something wrong, but being made to dance for the whim of another entitled jerk was not helpful to her recovery—at least that was what her therapist kept trying to hammer into her. "She was an entitled bitch."

Reba's job at the UPRC was to make sure that all the bulls, horses, and other livestock remained healthy during the rodeos. It wasn't supposed to be catering to the wives of the rodeo cowboys. She loved this job and was so thankful that she was able to be a vet without having to go back to the office environment. She just hated when the real world—and the Karens—tried to muscle in on her happiness. What was worse, her boss would take Karen's side. But Reba should be used to that by now.

Nowadays, Reba kept to the background during the events, content to let her bull-riding, bronc-busting baby sister, LeAnn, get all the attention. Her other younger sister, Dolly, was also front and center at the rodeo. Dolly was a marketing genius and a social media influencer queen who gathered up all the social media frenzy and directed it to the rodeo's "Next Big Thing." Luckily, that was never Reba or any of the other people running the rodeo behind the scenes. And that was just how she liked it.

"Reba," Diane warned.

"Look, how about I get Dolly to comp her a VIP package and a bucket of beer?" Reba's sister Dolly worked public relations for the UPRC, so that shouldn't be too much of an inconvenience.

"I suppose that will be all right. I'll have Vanessa pick up the passes at the announcer's booth in an hour."

"Great." Reba would owe Dolly one, but that was worth not having to see Vanessa/Karen's superior look of triumph. Reba hated people who didn't look after their animals properly. It was even worse if they had the money to do so, but they cheaped out instead. Maybe she'd ask Dolly to put a dead bug in the beer. Or even better, a live one.

"Also, Lou Porter and Shane Calland have just checked in."

"Already?" Reba frowned. Their bulls weren't due for testing until ten a.m. It was a little after eight now.

Lou Porter owned a herd of bulls that the men's rodeo organization had used before the merger. He was part of her family, sort of. He was Dylan—LeAnn's husband's—

uncle. He was a good guy who took care of his animals. Reba had never had a problem with any of his stock.

Shane Calland and the Viking Ranch, however, were brand new on this circuit. The only thing she knew about Shane was his reputation. About five years ago, he had been a champion bull rider and bronc buster. He had been hot shit, both on and off the circuit. Everything she had heard about him pretty much guaranteed that they weren't going to get along. With any luck, he wouldn't even notice her as anything more than an inconvenience to his day. She wasn't a stacked buckle bunny. She wasn't a rodeo princess. She wasn't afraid to get her hands dirty, and she had absolutely zero patience with a man who thought he was God's gift to women just because he could go eight seconds on a bull.

"Yeah," Diane said. "I figured you'd want to get a jump on the exams and have the rest of the morning free."

That didn't sound so bad. It would give her some time to check in with LeAnn and her horse, Garth. "All right. I'll head over to the bullpens now."

Being from Paris, Texas, she knew her way around the fairgrounds. When they were kids, she and her sisters had looked forward to this event all year. It was Christmas, summer vacation, and their birthdays all rolled up into one. Reba would be involved with her 4-H projects. Even back then, she preferred animals to humans. Loretta would be hoping for a blue ribbon for her painted landscapes or photos she had taken of the rodeo. Dolly would be doing interviews for her podcast with anyone who would talk with her. And, of course, LeAnn would be barrel racing.

As Reba made her way to the bullpens, she recognized a few faces, but kept her head down and avoided getting close to them. She hated small talk. Reba never knew what to say to acquaintances or people who didn't want to know the real answer to the question, *How are y'all doing?*

Reba had been better, but she had also been worse. When she had been worse, no one had wanted to hear about it. So, she had kept her mouth shut and carried on. Eventually, it had gotten better, but she had never forgotten her so-called friends who didn't want to hear about how she hated when she heard loud voices or still flinched when someone dropped a plate in a restaurant because of what had gone down at her last job.

It also wasn't out of the question that someone from Kilgore Veterinary Services might be around, and she definitely did not want to stroll down that particular memory lane. This was the hometown rodeo and town fair weekend, so they were bound to be here. Still, they'd be with the small animals being judged for blue ribbons and best in fair, rather than with the animal athletes that the UPRC hired for the shows.

So when she approached the pens where the bulls were waiting for testing, Reba froze in her tracks when she saw Dr. Kilgore leaning against the fence post talking to Lou. Why was Lou hanging around with a jerk like Dr. Kilgore?

Unfortunately, Kilgore turned to see her just as she was about to make her escape.

His face opened in a bright smile, and he said, "Reba Keller, is that you?" As he stepped forward, Reba took three quick steps back and slammed into a hard object.

Whirling with her hands up, ready to defend herself, she was surprised to see she had crashed into Shane Calland. Where the hell had he come from? She was usually much better at noticing her surroundings.

"Easy there, girl," Shane said.

Reba bristled, forgetting about Kilgore for a second. She put her hands on her hips. "Do I look like a girl to you?"

She hadn't meant to start something, but her toes tingled at Shane's long, slow look. She felt his gaze from the top of her head right down to the tips of her toes. She had to admit, it wasn't a hardship to look at him. She could see why he made the women who followed bull riders at the rodeo a little nuts.

He had sandy blond hair that was cropped tight to his skull, and flinty gray eyes that stared at her with an unyielding expression. He had a strong jawline, sensuous lips, and tanned throat that led down to a muscled chest that his cotton flannel shirt did nothing to hide. She allowed her gaze to dip briefly at his tight blue jeans, but then immediately went back to his eyes so he didn't catch her leering at him. It was a good thing he was rumored to be obnoxious, because if he decided to be charming, Reba might have been in trouble. She liked cowboys, but only the traditional ones that said ma'am, dipped their hats, and treated women respectfully. Lately, those types of cowboys been few and far between.

"No, ma'am," he drawled, tipping his hat at her.

Uh-oh. Reba felt a zing of attraction right down to the tips of her muddy boots.

Unfortunately, that distraction allowed Dr. Kilgore to come up close and Reba felt claustrophobic, trapped between the two men. She hurriedly sidestepped and moved behind Shane. It galled her that she was using him as a shield, but it was either that or run away like a scared little girl.

"Is there a problem?" Shane said, quiet menace in his voice.

Normally, the tension in his voice would make her uncomfortable, but somehow coming from Shane it didn't seem as threatening as when Kilgore did it.

"Reba and I are old friends," Dr. Kilgore said, smiling and showing off his perfect white teeth.

Reba resisted a shudder. He thought he was charming. He wasn't. And to make matters worse, he had wandering hands. Not that anyone believed her.

Reba wished she was full sass like her sisters LeAnn and Dolly. LeAnn would have told him in no uncertain terms that he was no friend of hers. Dolly had a caustic wit that would have eviscerated Kilgore where he stood. Instead, she swallowed hard and kept Shane in between them.

"What are you doing here?" she asked.

It wasn't much, but Reba was glad her voice didn't shake. She no longer had to be afraid of Kilgore, she told herself. They were not alone in his office. He wasn't angry. She no longer worked for him. Not to mention there wasn't anything around for him to start throwing at her. Still, her fingernails were digging half-moons into the palms of her hands, and she was sick to her stomach.

"I have a nephew who's trying his hand at bull riding

today. Maybe you've heard of him? Keith Kilgore?"

Reba didn't pay attention the rodeo cowboys, but maybe Dolly would know who he was. It was Dolly's job to promote these guys on the social media accounts of UPRC. If he was anything like his uncle, she'd make sure to stay far, far away from him.

"No," she said quietly when it seemed like Kilgore was waiting for an answer.

Not Kilgore's favorite word. *No, I don't want a backrub. No, I don't want to go out for drinks after work. No. No. No.*

"What are you doing here?" he asked.

"My sister, LeAnn, competes in the UPRC, too." It wasn't the complete story, but she didn't want to give Kilgore any information about her life. Otherwise, he might take it upon himself to come to the rodeos to see her. He had hated the fact that Reba didn't think he was as wonderful as he thought he was. After the incident, he kept trying to *make it up to her* by sending her flowers and trying to get her to go out for coffee so he could *explain* and *ease the tension* between them.

No. Hell no. Not then. Not now. Not ever.

"Reba, here, works for the UPRC. She makes sure all the bulls are in tip-top shape and haven't been tampered with," Lou said proudly.

She bit back a groan. *Thanks a lot, Lou.*

"Reba used to work for me," Kilgore said. "I was sad to lose her."

He was sad to lose a doormat who worked overtime for free, to make sure that he didn't explode all over the place Monday morning. If an exam room wasn't pristine or work paperwork hadn't been done precisely how he wanted it to be, he made everyone's life a living hell.

"You should get going," Reba said. At his upraised eyebrows, she felt a flash of the familiar fear, and steeled herself against it. He couldn't hurt her anymore, especially with Shane's solid presence in between them. But self-preservation kicked in and she modified her statement with, "The bull riding is about to start. You don't want to miss your nephew's ride."

She hated that she experienced a flash of relief when Kilgore's face cleared, and he nodded. "Yeah, I've been shooting the bull for too long, so to speak. Lou, it was nice seeing you again." He nodded to Reba and as he came around Shane, Reba took a step to keep Shane between them. "Reba, if you want to grab a drink while you're in town, the number is still the same."

You're the reason why I hate people.

"Good to know." She nodded again, not feeling brave enough to tell him to go to hell. Didn't they say that discretion was the better part of valor? Even if it did make her feel like a cowardly little wimp. She barely noticed that Lou had moved off into another area, leaving her alone with Shane.

"If you want, I can hang around and make sure he doesn't come back," Shane said.

For a ridiculous reason, tears pricked at the corners of Reba's eyes and she looked away, blinking rapidly so that he didn't see them. "That's really kind of you, but I'll make myself scarce. I don't usually watch the rodeos anyway. And he has no business being back here. I'll keep an eye out for him. If he comes back, I'll…" *Hide, like she'd been doing for the past three years.* "Go the other way," Reba finished lamely.

"I've got nothing better to do," Shane said. "Why don't I stick around anyway while you take a look at my bulls?"

"Suit yourself." Reba went over to investigate the bulls in the pen.

Ever since the fiasco with Hickory Livestock using performance-enhancing drugs on their bulls, the UPRC wanted to make sure that none of the bulls that were provided to them were tampered with before the events.

As she walked next to Shane, she couldn't help noticing that he walked with a limp. She wondered if a bull had ended his career. Reba wished she had Dolly's gift of the gab. Dolly wouldn't think twice about grilling him on every little detail. Reba preferred fading into the background. But she felt she owed the cowboy to be more engaging and polite. After all, he had saved her from Dr. Kilgore's bullshit.

"So tell me about your bulls," she said.

It was the only small talk that she felt comfortable engaging in. Animals were her favorite subject, after all. And it made talking to a great big hunk of a cowboy a little easier.

"We don't drug them," he said shortly.

Or not.

"I didn't say you did," she replied, testily.

"And yet here we are. Every time you people stick a needle into one of my animals, it's a risk you're going to damage them. All it takes is for the bull to move at the wrong moment."

Fuck you. This was what happened when she tried to be personable. She should know better by now to stop engaging with people who didn't want to believe that you were doing the right thing. Reba stopped trying, and just got down to business. Unfortunately, she was acutely aware of him standing close by, but at least it wasn't in an uncomfortable way. He really was good-looking. Too bad he was an asshole.

Maybe asshole was too strong of a word. He had stepped up when Kilgore did his creepy stalking thing that he always did. Reba would bet cash money that he would have tried to hug her if she hadn't kept Shane's big body between them. She grudgingly admitted that having a large, muscled cowboy on her side had its uses.

Reba collected blood and urine samples from each of Shane's bulls while they were still confined in their trailer. It made it easier to avoid horns and hooves if they got into a temper. When she went back to the lab, she would run the results to make sure that not only there weren't any drugs in their system, but also to make sure that the bulls were healthy and didn't have any transmittable diseases that could affect the other livestock.

Normally, Reba would be annoyed at having someone watch over her while she worked, but Shane was damned sexy and, even better, he any didn't feel the need to fill out the silences with inane chatter. And while part of her hated that she was comforted by having a big, strong man standing next to her, another part of her started to relax and feel safe for the first time in a long while. Reba bet that if she rubbed her cheek on his arm, the cozy flannel would make her feel sleepy.

What the hell was wrong with her?

Reba deliberately took a few steps away from Shane before she did something stupid like cuddling up to him. Seeing Dr. Kilgore again had really thrown her for a loop. She hadn't realized how very much afraid she still was of him. Reba had thought she had put it all behind her. It had been three years ago, for Pete's sake. Three years since she quit. Three years since he threw the jar. Three years since he grabbed her and kissed her. Three years since no one believed her when she reported him to the veterinarian board.

Reba put a hand on her stomach and willed herself not to puke.

She had shoved Dr. Kilgore away and would have cracked him one across the face if she hadn't been so afraid of him. Reba hated herself that she hadn't punched his fucking lights out. She ran instead and never went back.

And for the last three years, she had kept running. At first, from rodeo to rodeo and then from any cowboy who wanted to go out for drinks. She hadn't even gone out to a movie with a guy. Reba had kept picturing Dr. Kilgore's slimy embrace and it had spoiled any thoughts of romance.

She had thrown herself into her job instead of dating. And now, three years later, she was more settled in her career. Sure, she still moved around a lot. But she worked for a new company that allowed her to use her skills as a vet without being crammed into an office. She really loved working for the UPRC, especially when it had allowed her to concentrate on the animals instead of customer service. It was a lonely life, but at least it was safe. Or had been safe, until Dr. Kilgore decided to show up and throw a bomb into her careful existence.

Being a workaholic and a homebody had paid off, though. She seldom thought about that gross kiss. To be fair, she seldom thought about kissing at all. And Reba realized that was a damned shame. She had liked kissing. It didn't seem right that Dr. Kilgore took that away from her. She hated that he still had power over her.

Reba glanced over at the bull-riding pens. She should channel her inner Dolly and march over to the stands and tell Dr. Kilgore that she wouldn't be having coffee or anything else with him ever again. And if he put his hands on her, she would deck him.

Maybe she could ask Shane Calland to stand at her back, just in case.

As Reba collected the samples that she needed, she made sure she followed the procedures to the letter. The UPRC was adamant about these new protocols after Hickory Livestock doped up a bull and made it more aggressive last season. It could have gotten LeAnn seriously injured. It had only been a matter of chance that instead of LeAnn being on the bull, it had been another bull rider. Luke "Mick" Mickelson's leg had never been the same after his wreck.

After she finished up, she turned to Shane and said, "I appreciate your company, but I'll be all right from here on in."

"How do my bulls look, Doc?" he asked.

"So far so good. The office will run the drug test and we should have the results back later today, but based on what I see, there shouldn't be a problem." His animals looked healthy and clean. They were expensive animals, and it was good to see that Shane respected them.

He nodded and walked away without another word. She supposed other people would find that curt and abrupt, but as she watched him walk away with his slight limp, she recognized that he had just been done with the conversation. She guessed she could appreciate someone not wasting her time with small talk.

It let her get back to work that much more quickly.

Still, her gaze lingered on his strong back and Reba wondered if she should have offered to buy him a beer or something for sticking by her.

Chapter Two

Shane Calland

I F SHANE HAD still been bull riding, he would have just rolled out of bed and swaggered down to the bullpens so he could talk shit and check out which of the bulls looked like they were going to give him the best scores.

But those days were gone.

Wandering around backstage at the rodeo, Shane pushed down feelings of resentment and what he refused to acknowledge as a little jealousy. Did he miss this? Hell yeah. A part of him did, but another part sure as shit didn't miss getting bounced around on his tailbone by a two-thousand-pound bull or getting thrown off the back of a horse that didn't want a rider on top of him. Shane certainly didn't relish the memory of coming down on his ankle and having his foot go east while his body went west.

Shane now walked with a permanent limp because of it. On good days, the pain in his ankle made him irritable. On bad days, even he didn't want to be around himself. When it first happened, he took pain medication, but he didn't like the way it made him feel, disoriented and loopy, like he was out of his body looking down. Eventually, he just learned to suck it up, but it did make his temper short, especially with idiots. Even worse with idiots who didn't know how to treat their animals right.

Five years ago, he had been on top of the rodeo world. He had an exciting career that made him a boatload of money for doing something he loved—riding bulls. Shane didn't have to work his parents' ranch with his brother. He got to travel the world, party all night, and sleep with a lot of beautiful women. Then he had gotten married, and a bull had ended his rodeo career. Some days Shane wasn't sure which had screwed up his life more.

Abigail hadn't stayed with him to nurse him back to health. She had divorced Shane after his ankle injury assured he'd never compete in the rodeo again. She had been back on the circuit the very next season. He had stayed home to help his father and brother run Viking Ranch.

Eventually, Shane had convinced his father get their bulls into the small, local rodeos. After a few years, they had some interest with the bigger national ones. And then last year, he had scored the UPRC. It had been a great win for the Viking Ranch. They agreed to contract with them for their five best bulls. Shane's family still had some bulls in the local Montana rodeos and some of the smaller, amateur ones, but those were greener bulls that needed more experience before Shane could decide if they were destined for the spotlight.

This year, however, the UPRC decided to pull this shit with drug testing the bulls. What a waste of time—and it was completely unnecessary. But Shane wanted his bulls to compete in the big league, so he was willing to jump through a few hoops. It was a good thing that the UPRC paid almost double for the use of their bulls. It made up for some of the bullshit. Not by much, though.

By the time Shane unloaded his bulls and saw that they had food and water, he got a text from the UPRC acknowledging that his bulls were cleared to compete.

No shit.

He probably shouldn't have given the pretty doctor such a hard time. It just pissed him off that the UPRC didn't trust him not to shoot his bulls up with performance-enhancement drugs. None of the other rodeos did that.

Still, it hadn't been Reba Keller's fault. From everything he had seen, she was professional and truly understood the animals in her care. She was a head turner, and sometimes he'd find himself searching for her at each of the rodeo check-ins. One of these days, he'd ask her out for a beer. It was just that his schedule had been so hectic that Shane had barely enough time to get what he needed done before grabbing a little shut-eye and then hustling off to the next rodeo.

He listened to the backstage banter between the bull riders. Some were showing off for their girls, others were scrutinizing the bulls and bickering over which one they wanted to ride today. It all came down to chance, though. Every rider picked a bull from a blind drawing. They could trade amongst themselves, but that generally didn't happen.

The Viking Ranch's bulls that were currently on the roster for today's rodeo were his father's pride and joy.

Sverre, Ingvar, Vidar, Balder, and Torkel were his father's berserkers. His family was third-generation Norwegian. Their last name Calland meant calf and land in old Norse. When his grandfather had moved to Montana to build his ranch, he'd wanted to keep some of his heritage alive. All of their bulls had Norwegian or Old Norse names. Their animals were like family, so he found it offensive that the UPRC had to test their bulls for performance-enhancing drugs. His family had never resorted to that kind of foul play. But the UPRC almost lost a cowboy last year to a doped-up bull, so Shane understood why they had to do it. He just didn't like it.

Of the thirty or so bulls here today, Shane thought his were the most competitive rides, but he was probably biased. He made his way to the stands after getting a hotdog and a beer. Sitting down on the bleachers, he ignored the customary squawk his knee gave him at bending. He was interested in seeing how their bulls performed today and how they compared to the competition.

"Shane, how the hell are you?"

Still chewing his hotdog, Shane looked over and saw his old pal Barney Keating. Barney was a bullfighter, turned more rodeo clown these days. He dressed up to entertain the crowd while the younger guys chased the bull around the arena and put their bodies on the line. Right now, though, he was wearing Levi's and a T-shirt.

"Why aren't you in your makeup and heels?" Shane asked after he swallowed.

"I'm not working today," Barney said. "I'm here to see

my son win."

"What's his name?"

"Taylor." Barney pointed him out. "He's usually bull-fighting, but today he wanted to try to win the bull-riding purse."

Shane nodded politely. It would probably be a good chunk of change. Shane remembered the thrill of earning thousands of dollars on the outcome of two rides. He would have half of it already spent by the next rodeo, though. Damn, he missed being young and irresponsible. A part of him wondered if it was worth it to try and get back on a bull again. Then his knee or his ankle warned him not to be an idiot. One of these days, his brain would get on board, but not during the rodeo days like this one.

"I hear Abigail is back around," Barney said, with an elbow nudge and a waggle of his eyebrows.

"So?" Shane rolled his eyes. Abigail was always going to be around. If there was a rodeo, she'd be following the hottest new thing.

"Your ex-wife's looking good—that's all I'm saying."

It been a fast wedding. They got married in Vegas after he had won the men's finals five years ago. He didn't remember much about the wedding, just that Elvis had officiated. The honeymoon had been pretty good, but it hadn't made up for the months of fighting and nagging that followed. Since he hadn't had a lot of money left after his career-ending injury, it had been a fast divorce as well. Six months from start to finish. Abigail never looked back. But to be fair, neither had Shane.

"She's engaged to another bull rider."

"Who's the unlucky fella?" he asked, in spite of himself.

"Keith Kilgore."

The name rang a bell and for a moment he couldn't place where he had heard it from. Then it hit him. The creepy guy's nephew.

Shane grunted. If he was anything like his uncle, they deserved each other. He wasn't sure what the deal between the creeper and the pretty vet had been, but he knew the doc hadn't liked the jerk.

"Well, I wish them both the best," Shane said, and he did.

He and Abigail had tangled in the sheets a few times after their divorce. That had never been a problem area for them. But Abigail wanted to be married to a rodeo star. She hadn't wanted to take care of a man with a broken foot and a broken attitude. He supposed he couldn't really blame her for that. They hadn't married for love, they married for fun and when he stopped being fun, their marriage had been over.

"Your bulls are looking good," Barney said.

"Thanks. We're proud of them."

"Competition is going to get fierce," Barney added.

"It always does. But it's still early in the season. Any one of these guys could be in the finals in Las Vegas." Shane gestured to the bull riders who were hanging around the fences, waving at the crowd, waiting for the announcers to open up the event.

Some of them didn't even look old enough to be in the arena by themselves. And now he sounded just like his old man. Next thing you knew, he'd be starting his sentences with, *Kids these days.*

"I don't mean about the bull riders," Barney said. "I'm talking about the bulls."

"I'm not following." Of the five bulls Shane had brought today, Sverre was the only one that had never let a rider go the full eight seconds. The other four were tough sons of bitches, though. He hoped they all put on a good show. If the UPRC liked what they saw, it wasn't out of the realm of possibility that they'd ask for ten bulls next year.

"You haven't heard yet?" Barney leaned in, rubbing his hands in glee.

Shane had a feeling he wasn't going to like this.

"The UPRC is getting more paranoid about who they're willing to contract with." Squinting up at the sun, Barney shook his head. "Not to mention that they think it's a waste of time and resources to test the bulls before every event."

"I agree."

"But their insurance company isn't letting them go back to the way things were."

"Where are you getting this from?" Shane wondered how much of this was gossip and how much of it was true.

"One of the girls in the head office and I go out for drinks now and then. And she tells me things."

"Go on." Shane was amused, in spite of himself. Older cowboys chattered and gossiped like little old ladies at a bridge game.

"In the near future, they're going to have just three breeders supply them with all of the bulls."

Son of a bitch. After all his hard work and sacrifice to get this contract, it was all going to go up in smoke because some bean counters were trying to save a buck. The Viking Ranch needed the UPRC contract. Shane had deliberately not gone with the large or mid-size rodeos this year because he wanted to give the UPRC their best bulls. Although he hadn't burned any bridges, the other promoters weren't happy about not getting any of the Viking Ranch's premium bulls this season.

Maybe he shouldn't have put all of his best eggs in one basket, but Shane had wanted to impress the UPRC so they would contract more bulls from them next year. If they were no longer interested in the Viking Ranch, Shane might have to start from the bottom of the waiting list for the larger rodeos. He couldn't expect them to hold his place when there were several eager ranches waiting to step in and fill a gap. Hell, Shane had been one of those ranches, so he knew how it went.

"Seems to be a little short-sighted of them," Shane said, making sure that he kept the concern out of his voice. "Part of what makes things exciting is you get different types of animal athletes depending on where they were raised, by whom, and how they were trained."

"I think it'll go back to the way things used to be as soon as the doping scandal isn't so fresh in everyone's minds, but you didn't hear that from me."

"It's been a year. You would think people would have other things to talk about."

"Well, as long as Mick Mickelson is shooting his mouth off about his career-ending injury, it's going to be a hot topic of conversation. Although Dolly Keller seems to be on a mission to get things back on course."

"Who?" Shane asked.

"She's the UPRC's head PR person. She's Killer Keller's sister."

"You mean Killer Porter?"

"Yeah, she married Dylan Porter last year," Barney said.

"Are they both still riding bulls?"

"Just Killer. Her other sister is one of the large-animal vets who is doing the drug tests."

"I just came from talking with her."

"That's Reba. The whole family is named after country-western stars. Reba, Dolly, LeAnn is Killer's real name, and there's another one at home named Loretta."

"Any brothers?"

"Nope, but Killer's horse is named Garth."

"Missed opportunity," Shane grumbled.

"For what?"

"If you're going to name a horse after a country legend, you should have named him Merle or Waylon."

"You're going to have to take that up with Killer," Barney said.

"Maybe I'll take it up with her sister." Shane thought about the pretty vet again.

"It couldn't hurt to cozy up to the vet or to the PR rep. She could put in a good word for the Viking Ranch with the muckety-mucks making the decision."

"That's not my style." Shane hated all the new rules. They were doing just fine before Hickory Livestock had to ruin it for everyone. His father wasn't going to be too happy if Viking Ranch was nudged out of the way after trying for years to get in. Sure, there were other rodeos, but the UPRC paid the most and put on more shows.

"Every little edge will help."

"This is going to be a devastating hit to a lot of people if the UPRC only wants bulls from three breeders."

"There's more." Barney was warming up to his topic and sat down next to Shane. "If you get one of the golden tickets, so to speak, you have to agree to be exclusive to the UPRC for the duration of the contract."

"They better be paying damned good money for that, otherwise they're not going to get anyone."

"I don't know any details, but it's got to be pretty good because breeders are coming out of the woodwork to get in on this action."

"This has all the makings for a shit show," Shane said, his mood souring even further. They couldn't afford to lose the UPRC as a client, and they couldn't afford to be exclusive for more than a year unless they were being well compensated for it.

"I just thought you should be forewarned."

"I appreciate that," Shane said, making an effort to wipe the scowl off his face. None of this was Barney's fault. "The stock contractor that we normally deal with hasn't said a peep about this."

"I don't think they're ready to roll it out yet."

"Well, I'm not one for rumor and gossip. Is there anyone else I can talk with who might be able to give me some hard numbers?"

"I'll ask around," Barney said. "If I find out anything

more, I'll let you know."

"Thanks," Shane said. His father was going to be pissed about this latest development. He was ready to retire and hand the reins over to Shane. But if he thought Shane was going to have trouble, the old man would stick around— even if he'd rather be fishing in the Keys instead of running a cattle ranch. Shane could relate. He'd rather be riding bulls than pimping them out to rodeos.

"There's also been talk that the other rodeos would like to see the UPRC fail. Less competition."

"Now, that sounds like a conspiracy theory. Next, are you going to tell me that the 5G network is spreading the coronavirus?"

Barney eased off the bleachers. "I'm just saying. Keep your eyes and ears open. I've got to go back to Taylor."

"Good luck."

"We miss you back there." Barney jerked his thumb toward the chutes.

"I miss it, too," Shane said, admitting it aloud for the first time.

"Ever think you'd go back?" Barney asked.

Every damned day. "No," he said instead. He couldn't compete at the level he had been at before the accident. He had too much pride to even try.

As Barney walked away, Shane pushed down the irritation. That part of his life was over. He was now in a new career and as a bull breeder. He needed to pay attention to what his animal athletes were doing in the area. He watched the first set of riders try to go eight seconds on the bulls.

At the end of the set, Sverre was still undefeated. That bull brought in five thousand dollars per event because of that statistic. Ingvar, Vidar, Balder and Torkel also gave good rides. Shane charged fifteen hundred for each of them per event. Multiply that by twenty-five events and that was a big chunk of money his family would be out every year if they didn't get one of the new UPRC contracts.

Of course, they made good money in stud fees and selling champion bulls, but Shane liked going to the rodeo events. It made him feel that he was still part of the lifestyle.

Looking at his watch, Shane decided to call his father and see how things were going back on the ranch. He'd keep the news about the potential new contract to himself until he had official confirmation from the UPRC.

The phone rang forever. Shane rolled his eyes. It was a crapshoot if his father had left his phone in the truck, back at the farmhouse, or was now staring at it trying to figure out how to answer it.

"Yeah," his father's gruff voice snarled a second before it went to voicemail.

"Hey, Dad, what are you up to?"

"What the hell do you think I'm doing? Having a fucking picnic?"

"Are you?" he asked calmly, too used to his blustering to bat an eye.

"No, damn it. I'm at this freakin' computer trying to find who we have scheduled for Ragnar this weekend."

Shane clamped his hand over his face. "Don't screw around with that spreadsheet."

"I don't even know what a spreadsheet is."

And that was the problem.

"Didn't Rick print you out the list?" Shane was going to knock his brother on the head if he hadn't done that.

"I can't find it, and he's not answering his phone. He said he went into town for a feed run, but I think he's out screwing around with Lainey."

Probably.

"I don't know why he doesn't ask that girl to marry him," his father said.

Shane was not going to get involved in that conversation, so he steered it back to the bull they were currently hiring out to stud. "Is there a problem with Ragnar?"

"No."

"Then why are you looking up who Rick is bringing him to this weekend?"

"Because I want to know, damn it."

Shane didn't have access to the schedule from his phone. He'd have to get Rick to save it to the cloud when he got back from his nooner with Lainey Evans. "Do you have to know right now? I can make a few calls." Shane would look like an idiot, but there were only three farms that they had been considering. He couldn't remember off the top of his head who was set up for this weekend, though.

"No, I suppose it could wait until your brother gets home. But it pisses me off that I don't have this information."

"It pisses me off, too, Dad." Shane was going to have Rick put it on the fridge from now on. "What's Mom doing?"

"She's at her finance meeting. She's hoping to get them to raise the library's budget so she can buy some more books."

It was a little more complicated than that. His mother was the head librarian in their hometown of Charlo, Montana. She was curating a Western Plains Native American exhibit and was looking for funding for indigenous authors and artifacts from the Flathead Reservation. Normally, she'd be able to distract his father with another chore or something.

The problem was, his father was looking for something to do and he couldn't do the physical job of taking care of the animals anymore. Shane hated to throw his brother's assistant foreman under the bus, but it was better than having his father accidentally delete something from their breeding records.

"Did Tommy ever fix the tractor?" he asked.

"What's wrong with the damned tractor?" his father barked.

"You got me. I heard it from Rick. You'll have to ask him."

"That can't wait for your brother to get back. I'll take it up with Tommy. Now did you want anything or were you just wasting my time with this call?"

Shane didn't know why he even bothered talking to people anymore. "I just wanted to let you know that the bulls are doing well today."

"Of course they are." His father hung up on him.

Shane was not looking forward to the conversation if he

had to tell his father that the UPRC had changed their mind about using the Viking Ranch's bulls next season. Maybe Barney had been pissing in the wind. It wouldn't be the first time idle chatter was passed around like gospel.

Shane was ready to hit the beer tent and head over to the bronc events when his phone rang. Because he didn't recognize the number, he almost let it go to voicemail. But he answered it on his way to the next event, hoping for some good news.

"Mr. Calland?" a soft, sexy Texas voice drawled his name.

"Yes, ma'am," he said. It sounded like that pretty veterinarian from before.

"This is Doctor Keller."

Jackpot.

"What can I do for you, Doc?" Maybe he should ask her out to dinner, not because of the information she might have about the new contracts—or maybe not. She might know what was going on and wouldn't mind talking about it with him. The main reason though, was she was sexy and seeing her run from that creeper had brought out all his protective instincts.

"There's a problem with your bull, Vidar. He's bleeding from a cut on his leg and limping."

So much for good news.

"What the hell happened?" Shane barked. "He was fine in the arena."

"I wasn't watching. Someone noticed he was limping back in the pen and called me to check him out. I wanted to give you a call to let you know I'm on my way to exam him."

"I'll be right there."

Vidar was too young to go out to stud. He had the makings of a champion bull. Shane wasn't sure which bull he could even replace him with for the next rodeo. They had ten other bulls that were contracted to the smaller Montana rodeos. He'd have to go online tonight and see who they had available for the show in San Antonio next week, if worst came to worst and Vidar was too hurt to perform.

His father was going to have a shit-fit.

Chapter Three

Reba

REBA COULD FEEL the eyes of the bull riders as she approached the pen. She ignored their murmurs and whispers and focused on the bull. Vidar was a massive creature with thick, muscular legs and a coat of black and white fur. He was pacing, limping and kicking out randomly. His eyes were wild with pain. The staff had managed to isolate him from the other bulls, so she could treat him more easily. But not before Vidar had riled up the other animals—and they were making a hell of a racket. Why couldn't everyone just go away and let her work in peace?

They had one more set of rides to do before their owners could put them back into their trailers and take them to the next event. The bull riders were grumbling amongst themselves.

"Do you need a hand?" Ronnie Sunderland asked.

Ronnie was Karen/Vanessa's husband. He was her exact opposite in every way. Ronnie had made a point in coming up to her before the bull-riding event to thank Reba for looking at his horse this morning. He had confided in her that money was tight, but he was planning on using his winnings from today to buy the renal feed that Starshine needed.

Reba had sucked it up and called Kilgore Veterinary to see if they had any promotions going on. Since she knew Dr. Kilgore wasn't there, it had made things easier. The woman who answered the phone didn't know her, but she knew that the rodeo was in town and was pretty pissed that she had to work today. Reba had offered free tickets and Ronnie's autograph, and the woman had been able to come through for her. She had been able to give Ronnie a coupon code for a six-month supply.

"It's only twenty percent off," Reba had said, apologetically.

"I appreciate you." Ronnie had put a hand over his heart. "And Starshine does, too."

"Just keep it on the down-low." Reba felt a little guilty that she couldn't do this for every animal that needed expensive medicine.

"No problem."

In the end, Ronnie had gotten all the bull riders to sign their name on the program. What Reba hadn't known was that Ronnie was the number-one bull rider in the UPRC. Everyone was predicting that he would take the all-around and win the three-hundred-thousand-dollar purse in Las Vegas at the end of the season. It didn't excuse his wife for being a snot. But at least then, they could afford to keep Starshine in expensive feed.

Reba had taken the signed program to Dolly in the press booth. "Hey, I need a favor."

"Another one?" Dolly was dressed in tight black jeans and a sparkly western shirt. She'd topped it off with a cute leather vest and a matching brown hat. Reba felt like a frump, standing next to her. But then again, Dolly hadn't had her arm up to her elbow in a cow's vagina this morning.

"This time, free tickets and this at the gate." She'd handed her sister the program.

"Who did you piss off?" Dolly had asked, flipping through it.

"The list is long and numerous." Reba had shifted from foot to foot. "But hold them for Penny Markson. She did me a solid. It's okay, though, right?"

"Always." Dolly had given her a warm smile. "Even if we were at capacity, I'd find a way for you."

"Thanks. What can I do to make things square?"

"Well, we're sisters, so you'll never have to worry about that. But if we don't have to eat at Mom and Dad's again tonight that would make my evening."

Being back in Paris, Texas, meant that their parents expected their daughters to spend quality family time with them. And for the first few nights that had been great and then as the third and fourth night crept up, it just highlighted why they had all decided not to continue to live together on the road in the Winnebago once LeAnn's relationship with Dylan took off.

LeAnn traveled rodeo to rodeo with her husband. Dolly had an apartment in Dallas, and Reba had use of their parents' RV with the express instructions that no pets were allowed.

"Set it up," Reba had said. "We should grab Loretta, too." She hoped that LeAnn and Dylan would be able to join them as well, but Reba didn't want to totally abandon her parents.

"You got it," Dolly had said. "How does Hometown Buffet sound to you?"

It sounded like they would run into a lot of people that they knew. And Reba would have almost rather spent the evening with her parents, but she owed Dolly so they would go wherever she wanted. Dolly had said she would make the arrangements and all Reba had to do was show up.

"It'll do you some good to get out and socialize," Dolly had said.

Reba knew she was right. She was just worried that somehow Dr. Kilgore would show up and start his gaslighting schmoozing.

"Is there someone you'd like to join us?" Dolly had asked casually.

Reba wasn't sure why Shane Calland popped into her mind.

"No," she had said, too quickly because Dolly had zoomed in on her hesitation like a shark scenting blood.

"When was the last time you were out on a date?" she had asked.

Three years ago.

"I don't fucking know," Reba had said, hoping her sister would get the message and shut up.

Of course, she hadn't.

"You never used to be like this."

Dolly was too damned smart for her own good.

"Like what?" Reba had tried to deflect.

"You don't have to tell me what happened, but I know something awful must have happened."

Shock had rooted Reba to the spot.

"I know because I had something really shitty happen to me, too, and it took me a few years to get over it."

"Why didn't you say anything?" Reba had said, concerned.

"Same reason you're not saying anything."

"That's different."

"Is it?" Dolly had pinned her with a look. But then she'd relented. "I'm here if you need to talk. But you've got to stop this lone-wolf shit. That's not you. You're a pack animal."

Reba loved when Dolly tried to use animal metaphors. "I get it. I'll see what I can do."

"What worked for me is that I had to replace the bad memories with good ones. Maybe that will help you, too."

Dolly had left her alone after that. But her words sank in. Reba had a lot to think about. She had shoved all of her feelings under the surface while she dealt with a new job and new situations. But now things were leveling off and she was getting back to a new normal. It was time to stop letting Dr. Kilgore live rent-free in her head.

The problem was, Reba just wasn't sure how to do it.

Right now, however, she needed to concentrate on helping Vidar. She swung a leg over the pen. She realized that Ronnie Sunderland was still waiting for an answer. "No, that's all right, Ronnie. I got this."

"The bulls are restless," Keith Kilgore said, sourly. "I'm not going to be able to top my first ride if they don't settle down. It isn't fair."

"Settle down, Sally," Taylor Keating said derisively.

Reba recognized the other bull riders only because they had signed their names on the program this morning for her. Maybe as part of her coming out of her lone-wolf persona, she'd ask one of them out for a beer. Not Keith, though. She could tell he was just like his uncle. Unfortunately, there were a lot of assholes out on the rodeo circuit.

"I'm just saying, there's a lot of money on the line," Keith said. "This is bullshit."

"Who hit the bull?" Reba asked, pausing to sit on the fence. "If you're so upset, you should be looking to see who caused this."

"No one caused it," Keith blustered. "He got nicked on the fencing."

"I didn't see anything that would cut a bull," another bull rider, Nash Weaver, said, folding his arms. He had been shocked when they asked him to sign the program.

"What do you know?" Keith said. "You're the shittiest bull rider I've ever met."

"Fuck you," Nash said.

The conversation devolved from there as they compared dicks and insulted each other's mothers. It made her a little nervous to be around it, but none of it was directed at her. She hoped that LeAnn drew the name of a bull that wasn't agitated for the next round. But if she did, Reba knew her sister could handle it.

Putting that out of her mind, she turned her concentration back to Vidar, who seemed to have accepted her presence on top of the fence post. She spoke to him in a low, calming voice, hoping to soothe his nerves. "It's all right, Vidar. I'm here to help."

But he was in no mood to be comforted. He let out a guttural roar and charged at her. Reba managed to avoid its massive head as it slammed into the metal bars.

"He ain't happy," Nash said.

Reba hopped off the fence, her heart racing. She had dealt with aggressive animals before, but she hated having an audience.

"Got any of those tranquilizer darts?" Keith asked.

"Don't you guys have anything better to do?" Reba asked. Being watched made her nervous, and she couldn't afford to make a mistake around a pissed-off two-thousand-pound animal. She climbed back on the fence once Vidar moved away.

"Not at the moment," Keith said. He reminded her of his uncle in the way that he stared at her, like a shark with his beady little eyes. And when he approached her where she was sitting, vulnerable on top of the fencing, her pulse quickened.

"Fuck off," a deep voice snarled.

Reba recognized Shane's gravelly voice and was surprised that the menace in it didn't make her flinch. Maybe because it wasn't directed at her. But after the cowboys slunk away, Shane turned that steely-eyed glare on her.

"What the hell is going on? I watched Vidar toss Jennings on his ass and then stomp around the bullfighters for a few seconds. Marty Kreeger roped him and then they guided him back through the chute. Just an average day." Shane approached her, and she was surprised that she didn't feel trapped or at risk. Maybe because he had scattered the bull riders like a pack of flustered geese.

"I asked a few of the boys, and they said he didn't start limping until he was back in the pens," Reba said. "They think he got scraped up against the fence, but I didn't see any jagged pieces of metal sticking out. It's not bleeding a lot, but I can't get close enough to take a look at the wound."

"He's in a mood, that's for sure." Shane went over to the gate, but Vidar charged him, pawing the ground.

"Don't open that," she warned.

"Settle down, asshole," he shouted at the bull who tried to buck him with his horns through the fencing.

"Does that usually work?" Reba asked.

Shane ran a hand through his short blond hair. "It works when my father yells it at me."

It wasn't fair that a man that good-looking was also funny. It occurred to her again that the way to get beyond Kilgore's shittiness was to take up with a cowboy just like Shane.

"He's hurting," she said. "I've got a tranq to settle him down and take away the pain. But I've got to get close to him to do it. If you can lead him into the squeeze chute, I can put the head gate down and treat him."

"I'll go get some rope."

It didn't take Shane long to come back with a lasso. She liked the way his arms looked as he twirled the rope a few times while Vidar glared at him. Shane managed to loop it over the bull's neck on the first shot.

"It's almost like you've done this before," Reba teased.

He gave her a sour look. "I used to make my living doing this."

"I know. I was joking."

Shane just grunted. "Were you around when I was riding?"

"No, but my baby sister was. She was way too young for you, though." Reba arched a look in his direction. "And we would have hog-tied you if you had looked at her twice."

He just flicked a glance at her. "Don't believe all the rumors you've heard about me."

Vidar tried to shake the rope off, but Shane tightened it, wrapping it around his forearm a few times.

"Come on, you big bastard," he said and led the bull toward the narrow cattle chute.

When Vidar settled down, Shane climbed the fence to be in the pen with him. Reba tensed, thinking that Vidar would use the opportunity to act up.

But Shane muttered something that she couldn't quite catch. Vidar heard it, though, and flicked his ears, but didn't do anything else. Vidar balked when Shane encouraged him to move closer to the cattle chute.

The cattle chute was designed to hold the animal in place by enclosing it on three sides with adjustable panels that could be tightened or loosened to fit the size of the cow or bull. Reba stood at the front where the head gate was located. Once Vidar was in the chute, she would close it around his neck, which would keep him from moving his head and potentially injuring her.

But first, they had to get the ornery critter into it.

"Careful," Reba said, following along on the outside of the pen.

"*Áfram!*" Shane said louder, speaking in a language Reba couldn't identify. "*Fara heim,*" he continued. Whatever he was saying, Vidar was calming down. Eventually, the bull allowed himself to be led into the chute. Securing the back, so Vidar couldn't change his mind and escape, Shane said, "All yours, Doc."

"What did you say to him?"

Shane ducked his head and she saw a reddening move up his neck to his cheeks. "It's Old Norse. I basically said, let's go home."

"Well, it worked." Reba secured the head gate. Vidar pulled back and stomped, but was, in essence, trapped.

Moving around to his flank, she took out a syringe filled with pain medication. She plunged the needle into the bull's hindquarters. Vidar thrashed and bellowed, but within moments, his movements began to slow.

Crouching to get a better look, Reba cursed.

"What?" Shane said.

"A jagged piece of metal sticking out from the fence didn't do this." She pointed. "See the bruising here and the red welts?"

"What the hell caused that?"

"If I had to guess, your bull was whipped."

"I'm going to kill someone." Shane's hands flexed.

Okay, now she was a little freaked out. But she forced herself to concentrate on Vidar. Shane probably didn't mean it literally. She hoped anyway. She felt a familiar cold sweat go over her body and her fingers began to shake. Not now. She didn't need this right now. This hadn't happened in a long while. It must have been seeing Kilgore that triggered all these raw feelings.

"Hey," Shane said softly.

Reba clenched her jaw.

"I'm not mad at you. I'm sorry."

"It's fine," she said between stiff lips, but the apology helped.

Shane let out a big sigh and placed his hand on his bull. "It's okay, Vidar. This isn't going to happen again. We'll bring Pat or Tommy next time." He stroked the bull soothingly.

"Who are they?" she asked, mesmerized by the kind motions of his hands.

"Tommy's my brother's assistant foreman and Pat's one of our ranch hands who's good with the bulls. I should've been back here, but I wanted to be out front watching the rodeo instead of being back here doing my job."

Technically, his job ended once he offloaded the bulls into the bullpen and didn't pick up until their rides were over for the day. "Don't blame yourself," she said. "The UPRC was lax, and your bull got hurt on their watch."

"Yeah," he said, but he didn't sound convinced.

The twist in her guts eased, and she sympathized with the pain in his voice. He really did feel for Vidar. Reba felt a tinge of kinship toward Shane at that.

With practiced movements, she began to clean the wound and apply medication to prevent infection and to accelerate healing. The bull moaned softly, but he didn't thrash or buck anymore. Reba worked quickly and efficiently, her movements confident and sure.

Finally, she stepped back and wiped the sweat from her forehead. The bull stood still, his breathing heavy and labored. Reba knew it would take time before Vidar could be back in the arena, but she had done everything she could to ease his pain.

"He should heal up from this in a few weeks." Risking a glance at Shane, she saw that he was still brooding. She wished she had Dolly's way with people. Dolly would be able to cheer him up or distract him somehow. Reba didn't have a lot of luck with the social graces, so she defaulted to what she did best. She was a vet.

"If you see signs of infection, feel free to give me a call. I'll be on the roster for San Antonio." Easing up to a standing position, she went around to free Vidar from the neck gate.

"Thanks," Shane said hoarsely. "I need to get to the bottom of this. Someone had to have seen something."

"Just don't do anything stupid," she said, backing away from the banked rage in his eyes.

It stung that seeing Dr. Kilgore today had made her so jumpy about these things. Shane and Kilgore were leagues apart in their anger management and still, Reba wanted to run away.

"No one gets away with hurting my animals. Any animals," he muttered.

"Do I have to stick a sedative in you, too?" she asked, hands on her hips.

Shane's lips quirked in a reluctant grin. "Maybe. I hear you got the good stuff."

"Yeah, if you weigh as much as a bull."

Rolling his neck, Shane winced at the cracks in it. "I don't want to think Jennings did this in revenge for tossing him. But who else would do it?"

"Don't go on a witch hunt," she warned.

"Does this happen often?"

"Never," Reba said, feeling her temper begin to boil. She was going to report this to Diane and hopefully they could put the word out to stop whoever had done this from doing it again.

Crap. What if Diane didn't believe her? Reba didn't want to get a reputation here, too, of being a snitch or a liar. Both of which she had been called when she had tried to report Dr. Kilgore.

His wife's reaction had been the worst. She had shown up at Reba's apartment with her two kids in tow.

"Tell them," Jolene Kilgore had screeched. She had reeked of booze and her eyes were bloodshot and red-rimmed. The kids were less than ten years old. "You tell them that you're a lying whore."

She had tried to talk with Jolene, but there was no reasoning with her.

"You're trying to destroy my marriage and my husband's reputation. He's a good man. He's a great vet. You're just jealous because you don't own your own practice."

In the end, Reba couldn't tell the kids that their father was an angry old letch who liked to intimidate everyone around him. But she wouldn't lie to them either.

"No one believes you," Jolene said, her voice hitched on a sob. "I'll make sure you'll never work in this town again."

Reba had closed the door in her face. But she had underestimated Jolene's vitriol. Reba's car was keyed. She was shunned and gossiped about around their neighborhood. But when a dead armadillo appeared on her doorstep, that was the last straw. Could it have been hit by a car and wandered up there to die? Maybe. But Reba didn't allow herself to dwell on the fact that the wounds were too specific for that. She just buried the poor thing and then made sure her own animals were safe at her parents' house.

But Reba didn't really have a doorstep anymore, not one that she had for more than a day or so anyway. And her boss, Diane, hated anyone who abused animals. If worst came to worst, Reba could even go right to the top to Shelby Miller, the co-CEO of the rodeo, if she had to.

What if they don't believe you? a voice whispered in her head, and, for a moment, Reba was transported back three years, when one of Kilgore's clients had literally spat at her in the sidewalk. Buffy the Pomeranian had been confused at her owner's behavior and had barked at Reba as if she was the enemy. It had seemed like all of Paris, Texas had been against her.

Fuck it. It wouldn't help Vidar, but if it could save the other animals, Reba would do anything in her power to make sure no one else got hurt. Maybe she was getting a little riled up, too.

"Glad to hear it." Shane walked over to her. "Thank

you." He held out his hand to shake.

It was rough from working with rope and cattle, but then again so was hers. She appreciated the warmth, and that he didn't squeeze too tight or too long. A rogue thought tickled up as to how his calloused hands would feel all over her body and she nearly choked on air.

She took her hand back and resisted the urge to shake it out because it felt all tingly and warm.

"Are you doing anything for dinner tonight?" he asked.

Reba was wearing overalls that had seen better days. She probably smelled like a barn. Her messy brown hair was pulled back in a ratty ponytail, and she didn't have a bit of makeup on. Why on earth was this handsome devil asking her out for dinner?

"I've got plans." She sighed regretfully. For a moment, she thought about inviting him along for her family dinner. But she couldn't do that to a guy she'd just met. They would give him the third degree, and he'd run for the hills.

Reba realized that she didn't want that to happen. Shane didn't seem like the typical bull-rider womanizer that his reputation spoke of. She wanted to get to know him better. And if he was as good as he seemed to be, she was going to work on being more social. The thought of it cheered her up some. It would be good to have some nice kissing memories, especially with a handsome cowboy. She stared at Shane's sensual mouth and felt a little thrill of excitement at the thought of going out on a real date. "I have a family obligation—family night. I'd love a rain check though. Are you going to be around next week for San Antonio?"

"I'll be there late Wednesday night. Do you want to try for dinner on Thursday?"

"You bet," she said before she could let her nerves change her mind. Even if nothing came of this, it would be good for her to get out with someone other than family. Someone who loved animals the way she did.

"You used to work around here, right?" he asked. "Do you know a good steakhouse I could go to tonight?"

"I do, but aren't you sick of steak?"

"You're not going to recommend a sushi place or something like that, are you?" he asked with a slight wince.

"No, I was going to recommend this Brazilian barbecue restaurant. It's a meat marathon. They keep bringing you all sorts of beef, pork, lamb, chicken, you name it, by the platter until you tell them you can't eat any more."

"That sounds like my kind of place."

She gave him the address of Churrascaria and felt a pang of regret that she wasn't going to be there with him to eat way too much picanha.

Shane tipped his hat to her again and her toes curled at the admiring twinkle in his eyes. He could be a pleasant way to put Dr. Kilgore's asshattery out of her mind once and for all.

Chapter Four

Shane

SHANE FOUND CHURRASCARIA easily enough and walked right in. When he saw who was at the big table, he almost turned around and walked back out again. But Abigail had zeroed in on him. His ex-wife lifted up her wine glass in a challenging toast. It was that extra half a second that he wasted that allowed the other guys at the table to turn around and spot him.

Keith, Nash, Taylor, Ronnie Sunderland and his wife Vanessa, and two women he didn't know were just being served their drinks.

"Shane," Abigail called out. "Come and join us."

Bitch.

She knew he hated eating dinner with a bunch of people he didn't know or like. Keith didn't seem too happy with the idea, but Nash and Taylor turned in their seats with welcoming smiles.

"Yeah, there's always room for one more," Ronnie said, hopping up to grab a chair from a nearby table. "Scoot down."

Shane was about to turn them down and just go grab a

burger somewhere when the smell of fried onions, garlic, and fresh-baked bread hit him in the gut.

"It's all you can eat," Taylor said, grinning.

Shane reluctantly sat at the open space at the end of their table. Unfortunately, he was at the exact opposite side from where Abigail was. She looked like the Queen of Hearts, lording it over the entire group. She was still pretty, although Shane could see the years of living on the road in her face. All the makeup in the world couldn't hide the cynicism in her eyes and the twist of her ruby red lips. She still had a rockin' body, but Shane wasn't even the least bit interested. Even if her fiancé wasn't still glaring daggers at him, Shane had zero desire to see if Abigail was still an animal in bed.

He was currently distracted by Reba Keller's soft mouth and generous curves, not to mention the fierce intelligence in her eyes and the way she could make him smile with a tart comment. Shane wished he was the type of man who would have invited himself along on Reba's family night. At the very least, he could have pushed to take her out for drinks afterward.

But he figured that she'd be the dessert, and he didn't want to offend her by just offering up sex. That was the old Shane. Or rather, that was the younger Shane. He was now older and hopefully wiser. Yeah, he wanted to dance in the sheets with Reba Keller. But he also wanted to talk to her, too.

He didn't want to talk to his ex or these youngsters, who even though they were less than ten years younger than him, made him feel like he was their father's age. After

Taylor and Nash introduced their dates, Wendy and Becky, Shane placed his order with the waitress for a caipirinha.

"What's in that?" Becky asked.

Shane pointed to the menu. It said cachaça, lime, and sugar.

"What's cachaça?"

"I guess I'll find out."

"That's what I love about you bull riders. You're always willing to take chances on everything," she gushed.

"It's not that daring," Abigail droned. "It's basically Brazilian rum." She waved her phone at Becky. "Google, darling. It's your friend."

"And Shane's not a bull rider," Keith said.

"Not anymore," Taylor added. "He used to be a champion."

Shane hid a wince. Was anything worse than being called *used to be*? Where was his drink? He looked around, but the waitress hadn't even made it to the bar yet. It was going to be a long night.

"What happened?" Wendy asked.

"He wrecked," Abigail said.

"Badly," Shane added.

"I'm so sorry," Becky said. "That must have been awful."

"What do you do now?" Wendy asked, with a slight frown.

"Believe it or not, there is life after bull riding," he said.

Sometimes, Shane even managed to convince himself of that. Unfortunately, today was not one of those days. He wished his brother Rick was here on behalf of the bulls and

Shane was with these idiots drinking and thinking about victory tomorrow.

"The hell you say," Taylor said, taking a swig of his beer.

"What do you know about it?" Keith said. "You're just a clown."

"A clown who saved my bacon," Ronnie pointed out.

"And one who just might let a bull tromp on your skull if you don't stop being such a dick," Taylor said good-naturedly.

Shane smirked. He did not like Keith. At first, he was worried that it was because he was banging Abigail. But no, that wasn't it. They deserved each other. Keith was a turd in a cigar box.

"I hate that we can't smoke in here," Ronnie's wife Vanessa said.

"You can go outside," Ronnie said.

"And miss all the fun?" Vanessa pouted.

Yeah, this was fun.

The waitress, bless her, handed him his drink and he knocked it back. It burned nicely. "It's got a bigger bite than rum," he told Becky. "I'll have another," he said to the waitress before she had moved away from the table. "But make this one with the dragon fruit this time."

"It's not like you to water down your drinks with mixers," Abigail said, even as she swirled a swizzle stick around what was probably a Hendricks gin with lime and seltzer.

Shane wasn't going to get into it with her. Handling Abigail with a slight smile and ignoring what she said was the best way to defuse the situation. Six months of marriage had taught him that there wasn't anything she liked better than getting the last word in. It used to be his mission in life not to give in to that. Now, he just didn't give a fuck.

Although, he still felt the sting of betrayal every now and then. She'd left him when he had needed her most. Would it have killed her to give it a little more time? Abigail had upped and left at the first sign of trouble. Their marriage was probably doomed from the start, but he would have liked to have ended it when they were both on equal footing. Instead, Shane had to wonder if he was still riding bulls if they'd be still together. He didn't think so, but it niggled at him.

"You got it," the waitress said. "What can I get y'all?"

"Now, don't fill up on plantains and the rice and beans," Nash said. "That's a rookie mistake."

"I think I should just get a salad," Wendy said.

"You don't come to a place like this for a salad," Shane said. "You've got to try all the meat."

"What if I can't eat it all?" Wendy said.

"I'll help," Taylor said.

"To be fair," Becky said. "That's an epic-looking salad bar. I see shrimp and crab legs."

"Well, in that case," Shane said. "Let's go check it out."

Vanessa, Becky, and Wendy stood up with him. Abigail glared, and if she had been a cat, her tail would have been slamming down on the table.

Shane had to admit, he could have made a meal out of the spread at the salad bar but the servers walking around with slabs of tantalizing-smelling meats on vertical skewers had him selecting just a few pieces of seafood.

When he got back to the table, their waitress was explaining the process. She held up a coaster. "This is rodizio-style serving," she said. "What that means is that if the gauchos see green"—she held up the coaster showing the green side—"they're going to keep bringing over skewers of different meats to try until you tell them to stop by turning over to the red side. Now, you can change your mind after a quick break. Just turn it back to green and that will let them know you're ready for round two."

The gaucho behind her had a skewer of pink beef, just dripping with juice.

"What's that?" Vanessa asked, shuddering dramatically.

"This is picanha," the waitress said. "It comes from the top of the rump. It's tender. You'll love it. We season it with coarse salt and garlic."

"Set us up," Nash said.

"Enjoy." The waitress left, and the gaucho sliced several chunks off from his skewer and served everyone.

Vanessa quickly turned her coaster to red.

They had barely enough time to finish that when the next gaucho handed out sausages, and another one right behind them sliced off some chicken wrapped in bacon. The picanha had melted in his mouth and he wanted more. But he was happy to sample the rest of the meats as well. Lamb followed and then beef ribs.

"What's this one?" he asked the waitress as she served him his second drink, barely swallowing his mouthful.

"That's fraldinha. It comes from the bottom of the sirloin, near the flank. We slice it thin against the grain and marinate it with soy sauce, lime juice, garlic, and spices."

"I'm in heaven," Shane said.

"I'll get you some more." She signaled the gaucho.

"Well, they say the way to a man's heart is through his stomach," Abigail said. Her coaster was still green. Shane had always admired her appetite, both in and out of the bedroom.

Pork ribs followed, then pork loin, and by the time round two came around, Shane flipped his side over to red. Abigail gave him a triumphant look and accepted another slice of the picanha. There would have been a time when he would have flipped the coaster back to green just so she wouldn't win. But he was no longer competing with her, and, damn, but it felt great.

The only thing better was if he could have shared this experience with Reba. He wondered if she preferred the picanha over the fraldinha, or how she would drink her caipirinha. He should have taken a picture and texted her it, but that just wasn't him. Shane watched as Becky and Wendy took shots for Instagram and shook his head. He wasn't even on social media. He thought his brother might have set Viking Ranch up on there, but he'd never bothered to check.

"You never said what you did for a living," Becky said, having long since turned her coaster to the red side.

"I work on my family's ranch. We're bull breeders."

"Oh," Wendy said, her eyes sparkling. "Those dangerous beasts are yours?"

"Some of them, yeah."

"That Sverre is a bastard," Keith said, sneering.

Every bull rider at the table agreed.

"He is indeed." Shane raised his glass to toast his bull, but no one took him up on it. He drank anyway.

"I'm going to be the first to go eight seconds on him," Keith said.

"Of course, you will," Abigail purred, putting her hand on his forearm. She still wore her candy apple red nails long. This time, she had put sparkling gems on them that caught the candlelight of the restaurant.

"Good luck," Shane said, even though he didn't mean it.

"His price goes down when I do, right?" Keith said.

"Not by much." Shane shrugged. "If it goes down too much, there's always other rodeo organizations."

Abigail leaned forward. "So you're not on an exclusive contract with UPRC?"

He couldn't let Abigail know how much this line of conversation interested him. "Not yet," he said.

"Anyone ready for dessert?" the waitress asked.

There were satisfied groans at the table, but Abigail glared up at the woman. She didn't like to be interrupted.

"I'll have the tres leche cake," Shane said.

"Same," Abigail snapped out.

The bull riders opted out of dessert and ordered more drinks for them and their ladies instead.

"It must be important for you that the bulls toss us off more often than not," Nash said.

Shane wondered what Nash was getting at. It was asked casually, without anger, but he sensed that his answer would be important to Nash for some reason. "I've been where you are," he said. "No one wants to ride a tame bull.

You wouldn't be in this sport if you didn't like the challenge of pitting yourself against two thousand pounds of rage. But if you go eight seconds on Sverre and break his streak, good for you. I've got five other bulls coming up in the next year that will give you a run for your money."

"But Sverre can't command the same price once he's been ridden for eight seconds," Abigail pointed out.

"Depends," Shane said. "There are plenty of championship bulls that command a great price and they've all been ridden for eight seconds."

"That's the key, though," Nash said slowly. "You've got to give the cowboys a good ride and you have to give the crowd a good show."

"That's the name of the game," Shane said. It was a strange line of questioning that Nash was following. A bull rider knew these things. Maybe he was showing off for the ladies?

"That must be a lot of pressure," Nash said. "Your paycheck is riding on animals that you can't control."

"It's all in the breeding and the training," Shane said. "And my family has been doing it for years."

"My uncle is thinking of getting into the business," Keith said.

"Isn't he a veterinarian?"

"Yeah, but it gives him an edge. He can take care of his own bulls instead of hiring out. Although, he's looking to hire Killer's sister away from the UPRC to help him out."

Shane forced himself not to react. Not bloody likely, based on how Reba reacted to him.

"I think she likes her job with the rodeo," Ronnie said.

"She's a bitch," Vanessa said.

"Watch yourself," Shane said.

Ronnie glared at him, and Shane figured that it was his time to leave.

"Do you know this Reba well, Shane?" Abigail said with fake sweetness.

Standing up from the table, Shane threw a couple of hundreds by his plate. "She looked after one of my bulls."

"And Starshine," Ronnie said, turning the glare onto his wife.

"She sounds like a paragon of virtue," Abigail said icily.

"I hope not." Shane flashed her a grin and then walked away without looking back. He didn't need to because he knew she was seething for not being able to get in the last word.

What could he say? Sometimes old habits were hard to break.

REBA HELPED HERSELF to a big spoonful of scalloped potatoes, mashed potatoes, and French fries.

"Are you on the anti-Atkins diet?" Dolly asked. Her plate was perfectly sectioned with a slice of grilled chicken, a side of asparagus, and a lemon wedge.

"You mind your dinner and I'll mind mine," Reba said.

"At least put some meatloaf on that plate." Her other sister, Loretta, shoveled a spatula portion on top of her potatoes.

"I was getting to that." Reba added some grilled onions

and mushrooms before heading back to their table.

LeAnn and Dylan were already digging into their prime ribs. Their parents had decided to go play cards with friends, so Reba no longer felt guilty that they had flown the coop on them tonight.

When they were settled back at the table, Dolly took pictures of all their food and made LeAnn and Dylan pose with their steaks.

"No one cares what we eat," LeAnn said, between her teeth while posing with a toothy smile.

"Wrong," Dolly said. "Five thousand followers and three hundred likes can't be wrong. But we can do better for your site. Thank you for wearing your new Cowgirl Couture outfit."

"Thank them for the fat check this month," LeAnn said.

"Tell me something exciting about the rodeos," Loretta said. "Let me live vicariously through you."

"I had to put a bull on a diet," Reba said.

"That sounds thrilling," Loretta deadpanned.

"I delivered a calf that was stuck, using chains."

"We're eating," Loretta complained.

Reba shrugged and went back to her potatoes.

"You should come with us for a season," LeAnn said.

"Someone has to stay home with the 'rents," Loretta said.

"Why?" Reba asked. "They're fine. Don't let them fool you."

Loretta shifted uncomfortably in her seat. "What would I even do? I'm not an athlete." She gestured to LeAnn. "Or good with animals." She inclined her head at Reba. "Or into social media like Dolly."

"You could learn. I mean, I'm sure Reba could use an assistant," Dolly said.

"No," Reba said. "Loretta has delicate sensibilities."

"I do not," Loretta said.

"What would you do if you stepped in cow manure?"

"Ew, I'd throw my shoes out."

Reba nodded. "See? Why don't you have her work with you?"

"If she doesn't like bullshit, she's not going to like working in public relations." Dolly clinked glasses with LeAnn.

"I think I can handle hypothetical bullshit," Loretta said.

"It's not hypothetical, but if hanging out with Mom and Dad is giving you cabin fever, you're welcome to bunk with me in Dallas."

"Let me think about it. I still play around with the idea that I'm going to go back for my art history degree."

Reba shot her a hard stare. "Just not at Paris Community College, right?"

"Right," Loretta said. "Although, Professor Singer is getting a divorce."

"No, he's not," Dolly said, and with a few taps of her fingers brought up Loretta's former professor—and boyfriend's—Instagram page. There were several shots of him laughing with his wife and two kids.

"I didn't know he had a family. I had just wanted to forget about Derek."

Derek was her jerk of an ex-husband.

"I know, honey," Dolly said. "Singer was a rebound and a fling. You deserve better than both Derek and him."

"That's what Mom and Dad say." Loretta scowled into her plate.

"Well, just because they say things over and over again doesn't mean they're wrong," Dolly said.

"Maybe I do need a change of scene."

Reba felt bad for Loretta. She was the oldest and Mom and Dad had such high hopes for her. But she quit college to marry Derek who was an aspiring rock star. Only to dump him when he knocked up one of his groupies. His Instagram was a party page, too. Reba made Dolly check on him every so often. Reba kept hoping to see that he'd had all of his guitars stolen or that he'd come down with a raging case of syphilis or something.

Then Loretta had gone back to college and had a torrid affair with her professor. Loretta had found out at a school event that the asshat was married and had kids. So Loretta had quit college and was living with their parents until she figured out what her next move was going to be. But at least she had her art. She drew caricatures at local events and took commissions for artwork on Etsy.

"Maybe you could paint rodeo scenes and sell them at all of the venues we go to?" LeAnn said.

"I'd have to get started now to build up inventory," Loretta said, but she perked up and, for the first time in a long while, seemed really happy about something.

Reba hoped it worked out. "You can travel in the RV with me, if you want." It wasn't as if she needed all the room when it was just her and occasionally Dolly. "But we should see if Mom and Dad will relent and let us take Siegfried and Roy with us. Siegfried was her orange striped cat and Roy was her pittie. Both had been rescues that had been abandoned at Kilgore Veterinary. She missed her pets.

"That discussion is all on you," Loretta said. "I don't think Dad would give up his daily walks with Roy. And Mom loves to have Siegfried on her lap when she's watching television."

That was news to her. Her parents had been vehemently against taking in her pets all through her childhood. Of course, Reba had brought home everything from snakes to tarantulas to birds and turtles, in addition to the odd stray cat or dog.

As her family finished up with dinner, Reba felt like someone was watching her. Like there were two holes drilling into her back. She got a bad feeling in her stomach, but she refused to turn around.

"Dolly," she said and waited until her sister looked at her. "I don't want you to react. But look over my shoulder. Is Dr. Kilgore sitting behind me."

Dolly flicked a glance over Reba's head. "Not that I can see. Why?"

Reba had told everyone at the table that she'd seen him in the bullpens this morning. Dolly filled Dylan in on the history behind Reba and Dr. Kilgore. Of course, Dolly didn't know the whole story. No one did. And the more time that passed, the less she wanted to bring it up. But Reba knew she was just burying her feelings. Maybe like a bad infection that healed over, she had to lance it to get the poison out.

"I never knew he threw a glass jar at you," LeAnn said.

"Technically, he threw it at the wall. We didn't tell you because we didn't want to distract you on the circuit," Reba said. "It didn't matter." It still didn't matter. It was over. And things would get better as soon as they were out of Paris, Texas, and on the road again.

"It matters," LeAnn said, glaring around the restaurant.

LeAnn scraped her chair back loudly. And glared around the room as if she was looking for Dr. Kilgore.

"LeAnn," Reba warned, but it warmed her heart that her sisters believed her. Maybe she could trust them with the rest of it. Not tonight, of course, and probably once they were out of state, just in case they decided to make it personal with Dr. Kilgore. If they believed her that he had made a pass at her. Reba still wasn't sure they would.

"Let me check with Uncle Lou and see if he knows what Kilgore wanted." Dylan pulled out his phone and began to text. LeAnn reluctantly sat down.

"You don't have to," Reba said. She was so thankful her job let her travel from state to state, just in case there were any other Dr. Kilgores around. Reba was lucky that the UPRC had hired her on full-time. It was her dream job. It kept her safe and sane. She liked where she was, and she wouldn't go back to working in an office for anything. What she needed to do was to move out of her comfort zone and start reintroducing herself into social situations so her default move wasn't to run and hide.

"I'm going to go out with a new guy," she blurted out, hoping to change the subject.

That stopped the conversation flat.

"Who is he?" Dolly said, her eyes gleaming and her finger poised on her phone.

"Shane Calland," Reba muttered, already regretting saying anything.

LeAnn cocked her head. "Who's that?"

"He used to be a bull rider," Dylan said. "A damned good one. Now he works with his family as a bull breeder."

LeAnn nudged him with her elbow. "Grill Lou about him."

"No," Reba said. "No grilling. No stalking him on the internet. We're just going out for dinner in San Antonio. It's just dinner." She stressed the last part, but she knew she might as well be talking to the wall.

"Is he hot?" Loretta asked.

Dolly flashed her a picture from her phone. It was an older one from an old Men's Professional Rodeo Circuit program. "He was something else when he was riding."

Loretta gave a slow whistle. "He looks like a Viking in a cowboy hat."

He did a bit.

"Just be careful with your heart," Loretta said.

Reba nodded. All she was looking for was one good kiss. One that would make her forget about the last one she'd had to endure. She hoped Shane was a good kisser. And who knew, maybe it would lead to something else. It had been a long time for *that*, too.

The back of her neck still itched like she was being watched. Reba should probably call it an early night before dessert so she could be well rested for the drive to the next rodeo tomorrow.

"I'm just going to get some dessert. Anybody want anything?" LeAnn asked.

"No," Reba said. "I think I'm going to get going. I'm beginning to get paranoid. Maybe I should just head out to San Antonio early."

"You better wait until tomorrow. There'll be hell to pay if you don't say goodbye to Mom and Dad," Loretta said.

"Yeah, okay. I'll see you in the morning. I'll take care of the check and the tip. You guys stay as long as you want." Reba stood up and turned.

As she made her way over to the register, she saw movement out of the corner of her eye. Dr. Kilgore was smiling broadly and was walking fast toward her. Every instinct in Reba told her to run. But she calmly turned her back on him and handed her credit card to the cashier.

Hurry. Hurry.

While she waited for the credit card machine to finish processing, she risked a glance over her shoulder. He was almost upon her.

"Reba, what a coincidence," he said, reaching out to her.

Then out of nowhere, LeAnn flew at him. She had been carrying a large bowl of chocolate pudding in both hands. There was enough pudding there for their entire family, topped with whipped cream. It was too timed, too perfect to be accidental. LeAnn tackled into him. The pudding bowl toppled into his face.

"Whoops," LeAnn said, crashing down on Dr. Kilgore's leg so they both hit the ground. The pudding bowl cracked open.

Kilgore thrashed and snarled.

Dylan was suddenly there, helping LeAnn to her feet. "Darling, are you all right?" he asked.

"I must have tripped on that rug," LeAnn said with fake innocence. "I'm so sorry." She then grabbed a napkin off a nearby table and tried to mop up the mess while Dr. Kilgore sputtered and flailed.

The cashier handed Reba back her card. She gave her sister a grateful look and walked out of the restaurant.

This was bullshit. She should walk right back in there and confront Kilgore. Tell him to fuck off and leave her alone. But it would make an even bigger scene and she'd probably have to restrain all her sisters from kicking the shit out of him after they found out what he had done.

Or Dr. Kilgore could turn the restaurant against her. After all, he was a beloved local veterinarian and she had quit his practice. He told her before that if she pressed the issue, he'd blacklist her. He no longer had that power, but it still made her want to run and hide. Reba knew her fear was irrational. If she could only convince her stupid brain to stop the fight-or-flight nonsense, she'd have a better shot of standing up to the fucker.

Chapter Five

Shane

San Antonio, TX

S HANE PULLED INTO the AT&T Center, where the San Antonio rodeo was going to take place. He was there early, but it was still a nightmare to park and then it was hurry up and wait while they told him where to drive the trailer with the bulls. It was even longer until he and his assistant, Pat, got the bulls settled in their pens along with food and water. Pat took the trailer back to the parking area while Shane finished up registering the bulls with the stock coordinator. Once all the paperwork was complete, he texted Reba.

> *Are we still on for dinner?*
>
> *Yes. Where are you?*
>
> *I'm at the bullpens. Where do you want to meet?*
>
> *This place is a zoo. Meet me by expo booth #2. I'm just finishing up some livestock checks.*
>
> *Good enough.*

With a last look at his bulls, Shane consulted the map

of the center on his phone and headed over to the expo booths. Out of the corner of his eyes, though, he saw a flash of something moving by a few trash bags that had been flung against one of the makeshift buildings.

"Probably rats," he thought, not slowing down. But then he saw a flash of white and orange and he turned to look.

A kitten?

Walking over, he crouched down and, sure enough, there was a white and orange patched one, a black one, a white one, and a gray striped one.

"What are you guys doing here?" And then Shane saw the hole in the plastic bag where they'd ripped their way out. Some son of a bitch had thrown out kittens. Shane didn't stop to think. He picked them up and put them inside the wide pockets of his coat, two in each. He wasn't quite sure what he was going to do with them, but he knew he had to get them some food and water.

Good thing he was heading toward a vet.

"Hey," he said, when he saw Reba leaning against the exhibit booth.

She smiled up at him and then did a double take. "Are those kittens in your pockets or are you just glad to see me?"

"Some shitbird abandoned these babies. I know we had dinner plans, but do you think you can check them out."

"Of course. Come on, we can take the golf cart to the clinic."

"Are you sure you don't mind?"

"Not at all. Just hold on to them and make sure they

don't jump out."

"They seem to be pretty happy to be in there. Must be because of my fleece-lined pockets. Or maybe because I had some beef jerky in there a few days ago." Shane slid into the seat next to her and put his hands near the kittens while Reba put the golf cart into gear.

She drove like a maniac, not bothering to swerve out of the way if someone was in her path. Shane loved the look of absolute horror on the pedestrian's face when they realized they were going to get run over if they didn't move their ass.

The clinic was another temporary building. There were three people inside and he could hear walkie-talkie chat from a few other people.

"Let's take a look at the babies."

Shane put them all on the towel that Reba laid out on a stainless-steel table. They mewed in indignation until one of the vet techs brought over a shallow pan of water and then a few tubes of kitten food.

"We had some of these in stock, but it's the last of it. Just squeeze it and they'll lick the food out."

One by one, Reba weighed the kittens and gave them a quick examination. "All in all, they're relatively healthy," she said. "A little dehydrated and malnourished, but that's to be expected. They were lucky you found them when you did. What are you going to do with them?"

"Can any local shelters take them?" he asked.

"I can call around," the vet tech said.

"Maybe we can get the ASPCA to try and adopt them out at the rodeo?" another vet tech said.

"Get on that," Reba said. "Can we leave them here while we grab dinner?"

"Sure, but I don't want to leave them here overnight. We don't have the supplies for taking care of these guys."

"I can take them for tonight. Just don't tell my parents," Reba said.

"We'll stop by a pet store, too, for supplies before we come back," Shane said.

"Just don't be too late. They're locking us up at nine."

Shane glanced at his phone. "Maybe we should take a rain check on dinner." He hated to cancel, but he'd be worried about the kittens being stuck overnight.

"I got a better idea," Reba said. "Let's take the kittens with us now. We'll stop by the pet store and then head back to my Winnebago and order a pizza."

Shane couldn't believe his luck. Abigail would have had a five-star hissy fit if Shane had suggested something like that. "Are you sure that's okay?"

Reba squinted at him. "You're not one of those pineapple and bacon people, are you?"

Even if he was, Shane would have lied through his teeth. "No, ma'am."

"Good."

"Throw in a detour to the liquor store for some beer, and you got yourself a deal," Shane said. He put the sleepy kittens back into his pockets. "Let's take my truck. My assistant probably has it unhitched from the trailer by now." He called Pat just to check, and even though there were bar noises in the background, Pat assured him that he would take care of anything else that came up tonight.

When they got to the truck, Shane carefully took off his jacket and put it on the bench seat between him and Reba. "You're going to have to wrangle the kittens while I drive."

"We weren't expecting anything but large animals at the vet trailer," she said. "Otherwise, I could have borrowed a cage or a carrier." After locking in her seatbelt, she arranged the kittens in a furry puddle and stroked them as they settled down. "They seem pretty tuckered out, though."

He fiddled with his GPS until he found the nearest pet store and drove to it. After parking, he pulled out his wallet and handed her a hundred-dollar bill. The way he was dropping C-notes lately, his budget was going to take a hit. It was much easier when he brought in his own money, riding bulls.

"I'll stay here with the kittens," he said. "Is this enough to get supplies?"

"If I only get one carrier for them, yes. Don't worry. I'll make it work."

"You guys are expensive," he said to them. The orange and white one yawned at him. The rest of them were fast asleep.

Reba came back in a few minutes. The kittens roused when she placed them in the padded carrier. They gave a few token protests, but when she added in a felted mouse they were distracted enough to stop yelling.

Next stop was the liquor store. This time Shane went in and left Reba watching the kittens. "What kind of beer do you like?" he asked.

"The alcoholic kind."

"Be specific or I might come back with sour fruit-flavored beer."

"Beer-flavored beer," Reba clarified with a smile that made him feel goofy.

He couldn't wait to have a nice, relaxing evening with her. He made a beeline to the refrigerator section and grabbed a six-pack of an IPA and six-pack of an amber ale. When he came back to the truck, Reba said, "I ordered the pizza. Meatball okay with you?"

"Sure."

She gave him the directions to the pizza place, and he swung by there to pick it up and then they headed back to the parking area where her Winnebago was. Parking alongside it, Shane said, "Grab the pizza. I'll take in everything else."

He brought in the kittens and their gear next and then went back out for the beer. The Winnebago was larger on the inside than he thought it would be. Reba had placed the pizza on a table and was setting up the two litter box pans next to a door he assumed was the bathroom. She put out a bowl of water and kitten crunchies before opening the door to the cat carrier. The four kittens stayed in there while Reba served him up two slices of pizza, but as she opened the beer, the orange and white one poked its head out.

"What are you going to name them?" she asked. "That one and the gray striped one are boys."

"If I name them, I'll get attached," he said.

"They do grow on you," she said. "I might be able to

convince Dolly and LeAnn to each take one. LeAnn and Dylan live on a big farm with Lou when they're not traveling. But Lou might not watch out for a kitten while they're traveling to rodeos. Dolly has an apartment, but she'd be more inclined to get a pet sitter when she wasn't home."

"It might be easier to adopt them out to people at the rodeo event," he said. But then the perfect names hit him. "The orange and white one is Huginn and the gray one is Muninn."

"Why?" she asked.

"Those were the names of Odin's ravens. Thought and reason is what it translates to."

"I think that's wishful thinking."

"The two little girls should be Hildr and Sigrun, battle and victory."

"Those sound more kitten-related. Is this a thing for you? Giving weird names to your animals?"

"You need to honor the animal with a noble name to have them grow into. Or does that sound weird?" Maybe he should just stick to stuffing pizza in his mouth.

"No, I get it. It's like you wouldn't want to name a puppy Puddles."

Shane chuckled, feeling a warmth in his chest as Reba smiled at him. "Exactly. I want them to have strong names that reflect their personalities." He took a sip of his beer and glanced over at Reba. "Speaking of personalities, I have to admit, I'm really enjoying spending time with you." Being with her felt easy, natural, and right.

"I feel the same way," she replied, looking bashful. "It's

nice to talk to someone who loves and appreciates animals like I do."

He nodded in agreement, watching the kittens play with each other. "I think they're starting to show their personalities now," he said, gesturing toward Hildr and Sigrun.

They watched the kittens play, smiling at their antics.

"What's it like being a traveling vet?" he asked, taking another slice of pizza. He liked the Winnebago. It had all the comforts of home, as well as the additions of personality that were better than the generic hotel rooms he stayed in while he was on the road.

"I like not being cooped up in an office, but other than that it's pretty much the same. Although, I do spend more time with the animals than with their owners and most of the time I appreciate that."

"I hear ya," he said, clinking beer bottles with her. "Sometimes I'd rather be with the bulls than deal with my father and brother. Although, they're just as stubborn."

"At least they stay home. For a while, my parents and my three sisters were hauling it across country together in this RV."

Shane looked around and couldn't picture that many people living in such close quarters. "I think I would have forgotten my brother at one of the rodeos and then changed the locks."

"It almost came down to that. But then my parents decided life on the road wasn't for them and LeAnn got a boyfriend. So it was Dolly and me for a bit until Dolly got a full-time job in Dallas. She's got an apartment there, but like I said before, she does do some traveling as well when they need her to do live public relation gigs."

"It sounds like you're all close."

"We are. Being on the road brought us closer together. I was grateful that they were there for me when I had to leave my office job."

"What happened?" he asked, hoping he wasn't prying. He normally didn't add a lot to conversations, but he was truly interested in what Reba was going to say.

"Remember that guy from thc Paris rodeo?"

"The creeper?"

"Dr. Kilgore. He's an abusive prick. I used to work for him, and he made every day a living hell. Have you ever had a boss like that?"

"Can't say that I did, but I do have an ex-wife, so I can sorta relate."

"Did your wife throw things when she got mad?"

"No, she was a screamer."

"So was Dr. Kilgore. Only he liked to smash things as well. He was a wall puncher, for the most part. But one day, I guess he decided he liked the noise glass made when it breaks. He started sweeping things off desks and chucking mugs against doors."

"He sounds like a real asshole."

"He liked intimidating the staff. Well, one day, he let fly with a jar and it literally exploded when it hit the wall. I caught shrapnel." Reba gestured to her face. "I quit the next day."

Shane knew he didn't like the son of a bitch for a reason. "Did you press charges?"

"I was going to, but I sold out for a big check and a glowing recommendation." She shrugged.

"Is he still pulling that shit in the office?"

"I don't know. I know he always had a high turnover rate. I had been one of the last to go. I'm not sure if he found more suckers to work for him or if he made his wife and kids pitch in. This was the first time I had seen him in person in three years. Now, he's all over the place. I was pissed when Lou outed me to him. Now, I'm afraid that he's going to keep showing up to visit his nephew and make the excuse to see me."

"Has he got a thing for you?"

Reba paused. She looked down at her fingers. "I don't think so."

"You want me to beat the shit out of him?"

Yes.

No.

Shane saw the words flash across her face.

He was serious. He'd go looking for the son of a bitch. All Reba had to do was say the words. She reached over and squeezed his hand. "Kilgore's the type of guy who has to be the hero of everyone's story. And he knows he's the villain in mine. He tried bribery, gaslighting, and intimidation to get me to admit that the office wasn't as bad as it really was. As you can imagine, I stand by my account of things."

"As you should. Was there something else that happened?"

She stared off in the distance.

That was a yes. But he wouldn't push if she didn't want to tell him.

"It's over and I don't want to think about it anymore." She squeezed his hand again. "You can help me with that, I think."

"Anything you need."

He didn't understand the husky chuckle she gave him, but he was intrigued. "I hate to be the bearer of bad news," he said, "but you might be seeing him at the rodeos more frequently."

She made a face. "Why?"

"How much do you know about how the UPRC gets their bulls for the events?"

"I assume they take bids from the breeders and go with the ones that have the best bulls for the cheapest price."

Shane nodded. "It's a little more complicated than that, but that's the gist of it. You've got to have a stellar reputation."

Reba nodded. "Of course."

"Except now, from what I hear, the rodeo is thinking of changing their policy to only deal with a few breeders and your Dr. Kilgore is determined to be one of them."

Reba scoffed. "That's ridiculous. He doesn't know the first thing about raising rodeo bulls."

"I think he's looking to bring you on to help him out with that."

Now she snorted. "That'll be a cold day in hell."

"Just thought I'd give you the heads-up."

"Thanks, I appreciate it." She shook her head in disbelief. "How is that new policy going to affect your ranch?"

"We'll probably bid for one of the open positions, but I'm not happy about the exclusivity clause that they're proposing. So far, I haven't seen a contract and it's all just discussion at this point. Our bottom line is going to take a hit if we're no longer supplying the UPRC, but we'll just concentrate on breeding and putting our bulls into the smaller rodeos." He sighed. "It stinks, though."

"I hadn't heard they were going to do that. Any idea why?"

"They're trying to stop the blood testing for the animals. Said it's unnecessary if they're dealing with dedicated breeders."

Reba stared at her beer bottle and fiddled with the label, pulling it off in slow tugs. "I'm not so sure about that, but it could be that they'll look to cut down on the veterinary staff if that comes about." She made a face. "I could be out of a job. That sucks, too. This is the perfect job for me."

"Let's not go counting our chickens before they hatch. Or in this case, calves before they're birthed, I guess. I didn't mean to bring the mood down."

"It's okay," she said. "I'd rather be forewarned. It's just that I was just starting to settle into the job. The idea of starting over isn't really appealing to me."

"I think we're both on the same page."

"I've noticed we're a lot alike," she said.

There was a supercharged moment when they just looked at each other. Reba was a damned fine-looking woman, and he wanted to kiss her. He leaned in. She tilted her face up. He very slowly brushed his lips against hers. Time stopped. He lost his breath. Her eyelashes fluttered down. He kissed her again. It was sweet and sexy.

"You're a nice guy," she said, cupping his face.

"A nice guy wouldn't be having thoughts like this," he said hoarsely. His pulse was hammering, and his jeans were getting uncomfortably tight.

"You rescued kittens." Reba stroked his cheek. "That's superhero status in my book."

"I'm no superhero. Just a beat-up old bull rider," he said.

"Do you miss it?" she asked, tugging a strand of hair behind her very nibbleable ear.

"Every damned day." It must have been the beer talking because Shane hadn't realized that was going to come out of his mouth and the truth in it was raw.

He leaned back, getting comfortable on the chair. There would be more time for kissing later, he hoped. He liked getting to know her, even if she was asking some tough questions about things he'd rather not think about.

"Why?" she asked.

"The reasons have changed over the years. At first, it was the excitement. Followed shortly by the money. Then it was the lifestyle. My ex-wife was especially upset to be grounded at my family's cattle ranch. It's what ended our relationship."

"I'm sorry to hear that," Reba said.

"She wanted a husband who was a rodeo star. She had one for about six months. Then when it became clear that my ankle would not allow me to ride professionally anymore, she tried to be a rancher's wife. She didn't try very hard," he said with a small grin. "And that was that."

"She was an idiot."

"Thank you for saying that. How about you, has there been an idiot in your life?"

"More than one. My brand of idiots tend to resent the job after a few midnight calls to help a sick animal or being late to dinner because a birth is going badly."

"You'd think they'd know what they were getting into," Shane said.

"You would think that." She returned his small grin. "And the rodeo cowboys I see on a daily basis aren't my idea of a good time."

"Ouch," he said with a hand over his heart. "Are you saying I wouldn't have had a chance?"

"Not even a little bit," she said. "Then," she added on quickly.

"Then," he said slowly. "Well, how about now?"

Reba gave him a shy smile. "I guess we'll find out, won't we?"

Chapter Six

Reba

INSTEAD OF PAYING attention to what her boss Diane was talking about in the morning meeting, Reba was thinking about how she should have invited Shane to stay over last night. A part of her felt guilty for daydreaming, but Diane was probably saying the same old thing she said at the beginning of every rodeo.

Keep your walkie talkie on and your phone charged.
Stick to the schedule.
Call for backup if you need it.
If you see something, say something.

Besides, the job assignments were already on the white erasable board in their portable vet trailer. Their mobile veterinarian lab contained essential diagnostic equipment for conducting tests and analyses. It had an exam room with a platform for examining smaller animals and storage for their medical supplies and equipment, such as their portable X-ray machines and ultrasound unit. As the senior veterinarian, Reba was in charge of the bull testing again and on call for any horses that needed assistance. Dr. Victor Lance, the second vet, took care of the other wellness checks. The rest of the vet techs were assigned all over the place.

As Diane droned on about things to remain alert for, Reba's mind wandered back to Shane. She had a really good time last night. It had been a while since she had a first date that wasn't a torturous two hours of awkwardness. They had really connected over the kittens and talking about their families. And those kisses… Reba smiled, feeling her cheeks heat in a blush. She hadn't thought about Dr. Kilgore. She hadn't panicked. It was so natural the way his lips brushed against hers. And then they had just moved on with their discussion, as if they had all the time in the world to get to know each other.

After they polished off the pizza and beer, they played gin rummy while talking smack to each other. He had helped her settle in the kittens and Reba could tell that he really hated to leave Huginn and Muninn, or was it Hildr and Sigrun?

Crazy Norse names. Reba couldn't keep them straight.

"What are you grinning like a lunatic for?" Dolly asked.

Reba blinked. At some point, Diane had finished her speech, and everyone had started their day. Dolly must have come in when Diane had left. Reba shook her head. It wasn't like her to be lost in daydreaming.

"Can't a person be happy?" Reba said defensively.

Dolly stared into Reba's coffee cup. "Isn't it a little early to start drinking?"

"Coffee?"

"Whiskey."

"I don't drink on the job," Reba said primly.

"You don't smile on it either. So what gives?"

Her sister wasn't going to let this go. Reba grabbed her by the arm and tugged her outside. The fewer people who knew her business the better.

"If you must know, I had a nice dinner last night with Shane Calland."

Dolly's eyes grew wide, and she whistled. "Good for you. Just dinner?"

"I wouldn't tell you even if it hadn't been just dinner."

"It was more than dinner," she said knowingly.

Reba just shook her head. "We didn't sleep together."

"Why not?" Dolly asked.

"It was our first date."

"Don't tell me you're going to wait until the third date or something like that. You're not in high school, you know."

"It's not like that," Reba said. Dolly could be so outrageous sometimes.

When Shane had said he was fixing to go, he had helped her clean up. Then they had paused in the doorway before Reba decided to walk him out to his truck. Then they held hands and looked up at the stars.

After a few minutes, he had squeezed her hand and said that he had enjoyed himself. Then he gave her another one of those slow kisses and left her standing there debating if she should ask him to stay. She wound up watching him driving away and trying to work up the courage to text him to turn around. Reba explained all that to Dolly.

"It sounds really sweet. Why were you hesitating?"

"I'm not sure," Reba said. She had been asking herself

the same question. It could have been that she was afraid of freaking out about Dr. Kilgore at an inopportune instance. But that was just an excuse.

"Take the cowboy for a ride. No one says you have to get married."

Dolly could be painfully blunt at times, but she only said what Reba had been thinking.

"Maybe." Reba didn't want to make a fool out of herself, but she had to admit she wanted to spend more time with Shane and less time thinking about Dr. Kilgore. "Anyway, I've got to head over to the bulls."

"I'll hitch a ride, if you don't mind. I'm trying to get some interest going for Nash Weaver."

"Who's he?" Reba said, grabbing the keys to one of the golf carts that the vet staff used. The name sounded familiar.

"He's the worst bull rider I've ever seen." Dolly shook her head at her phone as she daintily climbed into the golf cart.

At least she was wearing decent boots today. Sometimes, Dolly came to the rodeo with heels and tight skirts. The professional cheerleader in her died hard.

"Everybody wrecks," Reba said. She remembered him now. He was the one who had been surprised she wanted his autograph on the program.

"Yeah, but as far as I can tell, he's never gone eight seconds. And he didn't exist before last year."

That did sound strange. "Is he someone's cousin or secret baby or something?"

"I don't know, but I need to find out before it leaks to

social media and causes negative press." She gave a big sigh.

"Are you all right?" Reba asked. Dolly usually lived for this shit.

Dolly rubbed her forehead. "I'm getting a lot of pressure from Shelby and Jackson."

"About this Nash guy?"

"No. About getting butts in seats. I'm trying to drum up excitement."

Reba looked around at the people in the arena as they zipped along to get to the bullpens. The rodeo hadn't officially opened but there were tons of people wandering around and she saw many trucks in the parking lot tailgating. She almost stopped for breakfast at one of them because the smell of grilled onions and sausage had her mouth watering.

"Are ticket sales down?"

"I don't think so. It's our first year as a joint company, though, so maybe they're not making the numbers they'd like. But the events so far have looked busy to me."

"Me, too," Reba said. "I've heard they're looking at cutting some costs." She told Dolly about what Shane had said about the UPRC only using a few bull breeders.

"That's just plain dumb," Dolly said. "No one is going to want to see the same thirty or so bulls rotating in and out."

Reba shrugged. "I'm just worried about my job."

"They'll always going to need a good vet." Dolly placed a hand on her shoulder.

And then Reba told her about Dr. Kilgore trying to be one of the bull breeders.

"I'll see if I can put a bug in Shelby's ear that we don't want to do business with the likes of him. I don't know how influential it'll be. But she should know the type of man Kilgore is."

And Dolly didn't even know the full story. Maybe someday Reba would tell her.

"Thanks." Reba parked the golf cart and pocketed the keys. "I've got to get these tests started. Come find me if you need a ride back. But before you go…" Reba said trying to sound casual.

Dolly put her hand on her hip, and cocked a sarcastic look at her. "Don't tell me you want another VIP package? It's not even eight o'clock in the morning yet. Who the heck did you manage to piss off today?"

"No, no. It's nothing like that. Yet," Reba added truthfully. Who knew what the day would bring? "Shane found four little kittens…"

"Absolutely not." Dolly didn't even let her finish before she started shaking her head.

"You didn't even know what I was going to say."

"Yes, I do. I cannot be responsible for an animal. I can barely be responsible for myself."

"I was thinking it would keep you company when you were back in your apartment in Dallas and when you had to travel, you could ask your neighbors to take a look in on the kitten."

Dolly was still shaking her head. "Sometimes I don't know how long I'm going to be gone for. Not to mention, I don't like any of my neighbors."

"Well, maybe you could travel with the kitten."

"That's a large pain in the ass. I'm sorry, Reba. I've always loved your kind heart when it comes to strays. And one day, when I'm a little bit more settled, I'll let you load me up with every half-starved dog, cat, or pig you come across. But right now, with my life the way it is, I wouldn't be able to give the kitten a good home."

Reba knew that her sister was wrong, that she would take very good care of a kitten. But she also knew that she had to respect Dolly's choice in the matter. The last thing Reba wanted to do was give Dolly more stress in her life.

"No problem," Reba said. "I get it."

Dolly bit her lower lip. "Maybe we could raffle the kittens off?"

Reba chuckled. "No. I don't want to adopt them out at the rodeo. Too much impulse purchasing. That could lead to the kittens being abandoned again. Don't worry, I'll find homes for them."

"You always do," Dolly said, waving before turning away to hurry off somewhere, while she typed furiously on her phone.

Reba wasn't too surprised to see Lou and Shane in the bullpens, observing the set-up situation as the other bull owners and the rodeo staff milled around the paddocks where the bulls were waiting for her and the vet staff.

She and Shane exchanged a glance. She gave him a tiny finger wave, feeling a little ridiculous. Part of her wanted to go up to him and give him a good morning kiss, but he was in business mode and she didn't want anyone to start gossiping about them.

Grabbing her kit, she headed to the first section of bulls

to get the blood samples she needed. She worked her way down the list and was just about done when one of the bull riders came jogging up to her.

"Ma'am, I need your help."

Reba recognized Taylor Keating. He had been more than happy to sign the rodeo program for her the other day because he said he was normally one of the bullfighters and no one ever asked for his signature before. He said he was trying to pick up some rodeo gigs in between bullfighting to make some extra cash.

Reba had told him there was a steadier paycheck bartending after the rodeos, and it didn't require risking a broken arm or leg. Taylor had just laughed at her and said he would probably drink up all of the profits. He was a handsome cowboy, with golden hair and dark brown eyes. Usually, he had an easy smile, but right now he looked worried.

"Can it wait, Taylor? I'm almost done here."

"Sure," he said wiping his palms on his jeans.

But Reba got the sense that it really couldn't wait. If an animal was truly in danger, she would never forgive herself if she had put off seeing it.

"What seems to be the trouble?"

"It's my horse," Taylor said, his voice shaking. "I think there's something really wrong with her."

"Okay," Reba said. "Let's take a look."

"Are you sure?"

"Positive." The bulls could wait a few more minutes.

"Thank you so much," Taylor said and took off at a fast walk.

"Hold on," she said. "We'll take the golf cart. It's quicker."

They piled in and Taylor gave her directions to the barn where he was keeping his horse.

"Can you tell me a bit about what's been going on?" she asked, keeping her tone gentle and reassuring.

"She's been off her food for a couple of days now and she's been restless in the stable," he said. "I didn't think anything of it at first. But today she's sweating and shaking and I'm real worried."

Reba nodded, taking mental notes. "Okay, and has she had any changes in her diet or recent medical issues?"

Taylor shook his head. "No, nothing that I can think of. She's been eating the same feed as usual and she hasn't been sick before this."

When they got to the barn, Reba saw that there were a few other cowboys lingering around. The air was one of nervous concern. That didn't bode well, and Reba was glad she listened to her instincts to come and help right away. When she walked into the barn and saw the horse, she knew she'd made the right decision.

"What's her name?" Reba asked.

"Dale," Taylor said. "She's gonna be all right, right?"

"Let me give her an examination." Reba was glad she always kept full kit with her when she was at events. In the back of the golf cart there was everything from chains used to deliver a calf that didn't want to come out of his mama, to thermometers, gloves, and other medical equipment.

"I need you to stand over there," Reba said, pointing to the front of stall. "Out of my way."

"Okay," he said. Taylor couldn't resist putting a comforting hand on his horse's neck before he left the stall.

Reba proceeded to examine Dale, checking for any signs of abdominal distention or bloating. The horse's heartbeat was elevated. She suspected Dale was suffering from colic.

"I'd like to perform a diagnostic test called a nasogastric intubation. It involves passing a tube through her nose and down into her stomach to check for any signs of blockage or impaction."

Taylor nodded, clearly not understanding because once Reba began the process, he gagged and turned away. Dale wasn't too thrilled either, tossing her head and pawing at the ground. Reba remained calm and persistent, speaking softly to her as she worked.

Finally, with a gentle hand and steady movements, Reba managed to pass the tube successfully. As she observed the fluid that flowed through the tube, Reba noticed that it was cloudy and contained undigested food. This was a clear indication that the horse was suffering from a blockage in its digestive system.

While Reba worked, she tried to ignore the chatter around her, but Shane's name made her ears perk up.

"Shand Calland's bulls are the best," a cowboy she didn't know said.

"I don't know about that," another cowboy she didn't recognize replied. "It's too soon to tell if his bulls can go the distance. This is his first year here."

"He's been around a lot longer than that," Taylor said.

"Yeah, he was a pretty good bull rider a couple years

ago," someone else said.

"Now, I remember him. He sure knew how to party. He was always good for buying a round or two."

"When he was in the bar," another cowboy said, elbowing his friend. "Most the time he had girls all over him, and it wasn't drinking he was interested in doing."

Reba made a face as the boys laughed and jostled each other. It wasn't as if she didn't know what Shane's reputation was. But it was still a little annoying to hear about it through the bro-dude network.

"Okay, I'm pretty sure Dale has colic," Reba interrupted, turning to Taylor to explain the findings. "I'd like to perform rectal palpation next. It involves inserting my gloved hand through the horse's rectum to feel for any abnormalities."

"I need to…" Taylor gagged again.

"It's okay," Reba said. "I got this."

As she performed the rectal palpation, Dale was clearly uncomfortable, shifting her weight and tossing her head. Reba worked quickly and methodically, feeling for any signs of impaction or other obstructions.

After completing her assessment, Reba explained to Taylor the next steps in treating the colic. As she administered pain medication and fluids through an intravenous drip and closely monitored Dale's vital signs, the conversation started up again.

"One time on a bet," Taylor said, "Shane and my dad climbed up on the roof of the Cheyenne Bank and took pictures of themselves riding the bronze horse statue up there."

Reba's laugh snorted out of her unexpectedly.

"Pics or it didn't happen."

"Yeah, I don't remember seeing that on Insta or Snap-chat."

Reba finished up with Dale, disposing the arm sleeve glove into the trash. She gave Taylor a pat on the chest. "She should be okay but let me give you my number in case something else goes wrong. If I don't answer right away, I'm not ignoring you. I probably just have my hands full, probably literally, with some shit."

Taylor cracked a smile and programmed her number into his phone. "I really appreciate this, Doc."

"I'll check in on her later, too." Reba cleaned up a bit more from the outside spigot and then put her equipment away. She took the golf cart back to the bullpens and saw that the bulls had all been marked as being tested.

"What the heck?" She got on the walkie-talkie. "Who finished up for me in the bullpens?"

The radio hissed static and one of the vet techs picked up the call. "I thought you had missed a few, so I sent Doctor Victor over to finish."

"I just stepped away for a moment," Reba said, ticked off.

"You were gone over an hour and we had to get these tests in. I'm so sorry," the tech said, sounding panicked.

"That was because I was busy looking at one of the cowboy's horses who was suffering from colic."

"I'm not accusing you of not doing the job." Now, the vet tech sounded scared.

Reba cursed to herself. "Shit, I know that. I'm not mad

at you. I'm mad at myself for not calling in and letting you guys know where I was. You did a great job." Reba knew more than anyone how hard the vet techs worked, and she also knew that they didn't need shit from doctors having a snit. "You got the job done. That was great. I didn't want to cause Victor or anyone else any more work."

"He was fine with it," the tech said. "We're all part of a team here. You would help him out in a second, if he needed it."

That was true, but Reba wasn't used to the teamwork. It wasn't as if she had any altercations with any of the other doctors. And her boss, Diane, was always fair. It would take more time, Reba guessed, until she stopped second-guessing herself and getting defensive. She hadn't told her about her suspicions that Vidar had been whipped. What if Diane had investigated it and a bull rider contradicted her and said it was a fence injury? Reba didn't want to be thought of as a troublemaker. If it happened again, she would definitely say something. Or if she had better proof of it being a whip wound.

She was disappointed in herself. She should have filed a report. This cowardice was another thing to thank Dr. Kilgore for. Reba was just glad she was able to assure the vet tech that she hadn't been angry with her.

The rest of the morning was spent doing routine check-ups and confirming the bulls' test results. They were good to go, and she was on to her next project. Reba made it a point to catch up to LeAnn and Garth before their events.

"How's my best boy doing?" Reba said, giving Garth's mane a loving stroke. She touched her forehead to his when the horse came in to nuzzle her fingers. "I don't have anything for you. You're going to have to wait until you're done with work."

"That's what I keep telling him," LeAnn said, smiling as she came up to them.

She looked sharp, like she always did. Her new duds from Cowboy Couture, however, brought her star level up a few notches as Dolly would say. While Reba didn't miss being crammed into the RV with her sisters, she did miss seeing her baby sister shine in the arena.

"I know you're busy," Reba said. "But I wanted to ask you a question."

"If it's about taking the kittens, we can't do that."

Telephone, telegraph, tell Dolly. "You could at least let me get the sales pitch out of the way."

LeAnn shook her head vigorously. "Hell no. I'd wind up taking them if I did. You know I love kittens. I'm not even going to go and visit them."

"They are really cute," Reba said. "I'm on my way over there right now to let them out and play with them a little bit. I want to make sure they have enough food and water to get through the long day until I get back."

"Mom and Dad are going to kill you if they wreck the Winnebago."

"They'll be fine. They're in a carrier." Reba felt a little guilty about that, but it was the safest place for them. And as long as she kept checking on them, and taking them out throughout the day, they should be all right. The RV was climate-controlled so they wouldn't be out in the Texas heat. They were safe, well fed, and sitting on soft towels.

Still, Reba would make a few extra trips to the RV and back on the golf cart throughout the rodeo to check on them. "Are you sure you don't want to see them? Hold them?"

"No," LeAnn said, but she looked tempted. "I have to get ready for my ride."

"What about Dylan?" LeAnn's husband couldn't deny her anything.

"Dylan would cave, too," LeAnn said. "He's afraid that the barn cats wouldn't take to the babies. And Lou isn't going to pay any attention to that sort of thing, even if he was around."

"What about his wife?"

"She's too busy to have kittens underfoot."

Reba nodded. "Sure, I understand.

Leanne leaned in conspiratorially. "Take lots of pictures of them, though."

"I will."

"Are you going to watch my ride today?" Leanne asked.

"Sorry, all my free time and breaks are going to be spent taking care of the kittens," Reba said apologetically. "But I know you'll do great. Any concerns about the bulls or the broncs?"

LeAnn shook her head. "Competition is fierce, but I got my eyes on the prize."

"You always do," Reba said, giving her baby sister a big hug. "Good luck and give them hell."

Reba took a turn by the RV to check on the kittens before going back to work.

Chapter Seven

JACKSON BLEVINS SPUN around in his chair so he could look out over the city. He had wanted to move the headquarters to Dallas, but according to their accountant Benny, "they couldn't afford it." Which was bullshit, but he was willing to bide his time.

He called down to the ticket office. "How are we doing in San Antonio?"

It wasn't capacity, but it wasn't a shitty number.

"We can do better," he said. "Release a few tickets to the local radio stations and throw in a meet-and-greet with Ronnie. See if we can get some buzz that way."

"We've already done that, sir."

"Then get Dolly Keller on the internet and have her work her magic. I want another hundred tickets sold for tomorrow. And I want it done by five p.m."

"Yes, sir."

Incompetent. At this rate, he was going to have to put some more money in his Grand Cayman bank account to prepare for when this thing went tits-up. It was a shame, too. He really liked the rodeo.

He made another call. This one to his bookie.

"Put me down for ten thousand dollars that Sverre stays undefeated."

"You know something I don't know?"

"I know that bull is a contender." Jackson hung up. That, and he had a man on the inside who was going to make sure that the bull was drugged into a frenzy. No one, no matter how good a bull rider they were, was going to stay eight seconds on that beast.

And he was going to make Sverre the star attraction. The unrideable bull. That should get them coming into the rodeo in droves. He took out his special box again and did another bump. This was the good stuff, and he was brilliant for figuring out how to move the product across the borders. Even the most dedicated border agent didn't want to root around in literal bull shit.

His next call was to Dolly Keller.

"Hi, Mr. Blevins. Don't worry, I've got a plan to get those hundred tickets sold." She sounded out of breath. He wondered if she had been practicing her cheerleading skills. She used to be a Dallas Cowboys cheerleader. It was one of the reasons why he'd hired her.

"I've got every bit of faith in you, Dolly. I'm calling because I want you to set up a public relations campaign for one of our star athletes."

"Don't tell me it's Nash Weaver," she said sourly.

"Who?"

"Exactly," she said.

"No. This is for one of our four-legged athletes. Have you heard of a bull named Sverre?"

"Yeah, he's undefeated."

"We want to promote him as a headliner. Come see the beast who can't be tamed. Shit like that. I want to see it on posters and all over the internet. I'd prefer not to spend ad money, so make him go viral."

"Just like that," she said flatly. "Have it go viral, you say."

"It's what I hired you for. Don't disappoint me." Jackson hung up.

And now it was time for a little R&R. He did another line. "Debbi," he said into his intercom to his secretary. "Get your pretty little ass in here. And you better be wearing those heels I bought for you."

Reba

San Antonio, TX—AT&T Center

WHILE REBA MADE her rounds throughout the day checking on the animals, she kept her eye out for Shane, but either he was too busy or wasn't around. She did notice Nash Weaver, Dolly's mysterious cowboy, wandering around places cowboys shouldn't be. She pulled up beside him in a golf cart to confront him.

"Are you lost, Nash?" she asked.

Nash turned and gave her a slow smile. He was another handsome devil, with deep green eyes and wavy black hair. Maybe that was why he was one of the headliners in the UPRC's program.

Reba didn't know if he could ride a bull worth a damn,

and according to Dolly he couldn't, but when he smiled like that, she could see why some women would buy a ticket. Fortunately, she was immune to that sort of flash and swagger. She was going to stare at him with what she hoped was a stern face, until he blurted out what the heck he was doing in this area. The look was usually reserved for negligent owners or animal handlers.

"I was just checking out the competition." Nash inclined his head toward the bulls.

"You had your chance to take a look at the during the lottery. Are you not satisfied with the two bulls that you drew to ride?" she asked.

Nash grimaced. "It's all the same to me."

Reba wondered about that. Most of the bull riders had the stats down on every bull and spent hours yakking about it.

"What do you mean?" Reba said, patting the seat next to her. "Come on, we have to get you out of here before you get into trouble."

Nash swung himself into the seat next to her. "Sorry about that. I tend to wander."

"And not look at signs that say keep out?"

"I always assume the signs don't apply to me." He gave her that smile again.

Yeah, she was definitely immune to his charms. When he saw that it wasn't working, Nash cleared his throat and said, "I'm just trying to figure out how to put in a better showing."

Now that she could understand. "Yeah, Dolly tells me your scores have been pretty dismal."

He perked up a little bit at that, which was surprising. Normally, bull riders didn't like to be reminded when they sucked. "Dolly mentioned me?"

"Yeah," Reba said.

So that was why he was so happy. She looked at him again. He and Dolly would make a good couple. Nash looked like he was more of a fashion model than a bull rider anyway.

"You know, you should seek her out. Her specialty is getting an internet buzz for the riders. It won't help you ride any better, but the more fans you have cheering for you in the crowd, the more encouraging it is. At least, that's what my sister LeAnn says."

"Yeah," he said, taking off his hat and staring into it. "I don't really like social media all that much."

So much for being perfect for Dolly. "Dolly lives for it," Reba said as she drove them back out to the main area. "But if you're looking to get better at bull riding, you should go to Trent Campbell. He's got a bull-riding school in Last Stand, Texas."

"I heard good things about him. Maybe I'll do that."

She pulled the golf cart to a stop. "Keep out of trouble," Reba said. "Stay out of restricted areas. If I catch you again back there, I'm going to have to say something. I don't want to get you in trouble."

"I appreciate that, ma'am," he said, getting out of the golf cart.

Reba thought for a moment about playing matchmaker, but then decided if Dolly couldn't take on the responsibility of a kitten right now, then she probably couldn't take on the responsibility of a boyfriend either.

The rest of the day passed uneventfully, and she couldn't wait to get back to the RV, take a shower and see her kittens. Maybe not in that order. After her shower, Reba sat on the couch and played with the kittens. She called up her sister Loretta, who was back home in Paris, Texas, with their parents.

"Have you given any thought about coming on the road with us?" Reba asked.

"Yeah," Loretta said. "I'm going to do it next season, if you don't mind."

"I don't mind. There's more than enough room in the Winnebago for you. How much artwork are you going to bring?"

"It depends on how much I can get done between now and then. But we'll figure it out. Even if I have to rent a trailer for it all."

"Whoa," Reba said. "How much are you planning on painting?"

"I've been using it as a stress release lately," Loretta said, laughing. "How much tonnage can the Winnebago pull?"

"If worst comes to worst, we can always hook something up to LeAnn or Dolly's pickup trucks."

"I'm looking forward to it." Loretta lowered her voice. "I really need to get away."

Reba could definitely relate. "While I got you on the phone…" she said.

"No, we can't take the kittens. No, Mom and Dad don't know yet. You better get rid of them before they find out."

"How are they going to find out?" Reba said testily, not surprised that Loretta already knew about the kittens.

"All it's going to take is one accident. If Mom smells cat pee, you're history."

"I'm trying to find homes for them," Reba said quietly. "Good homes."

"Well, it can't be with any of us. We're at maximum pet capacity."

Not even close, but Reba had to try anyway. There were plenty of shelters along the rodeo routes, and she might be able to see if one of the other vets knew of a family who was looking to adopt a kitten. But to be honest, she missed having pets with her and she wanted to enjoy the kittens for a little bit longer. She told herself that she was just waiting for the right home.

"I've got to go," Reba said. "I've got another call coming through." It was Shane.

"Okay," Loretta said. "I'll talk to you later."

As Reba switched over to answer Shane's call, she marveled at the little butterflies in her stomach. What was she—a teenager again? Still, his deep gravelly voice made her smile and she hoped that she'd be able to get a second shot at a goodnight kiss.

"Have you eaten yet?" Shane asked.

"No, not yet," she said.

"Good. I picked up some barbecue. I was hoping for a chance to come over and see the kittens."

"Absolutely, as long as you brought cornbread."

"Do I look like an amateur to you?"

"I'm sorry I doubted you."

There was a knock on the RV door. "One second," she said. Reba peeked out and saw Shane standing there with a bucket of chicken under his arm and a six-pack of beer in his other hand. Smiling, she hung up and opened the door for him.

"What would you have done if I wasn't home?" she asked as he stepped into the RV.

"Ate all the chicken by myself."

"I was looking for you today," she said, watching the doorway in case the kittens decided to make a break for it.

Luckily, they were racing around by her bedroom. One. Two. Three. Four. All accounted for. She closed the door firmly and got out two plates and some silverware.

"I was in and out of the arena all day today. Pat was handling the bulls, for the most part. There weren't any more incidents, right?"

Reba thought for a second. "Not that I've heard." She thought about seeing Nash Weaver where he shouldn't be but didn't want to make an accusation without any more proof. If she found him there again, she'd mention it to Shane.

Shane grunted. "Good. Maybe it was a one-time thing."

"No luck of finding out who whipped Vidar?"

Shane grimly shook his head. "It wasn't Jennings. He was the first one I thought of. You know, wanting to get revenge against the bull who threw him. Not only did he have an alibi, but it's just not in him to hurt an animal."

"I hope it's not in any of those guys to hurt an animal," Reba said, but she knew better. "Does anybody have a grudge against you?"

"That was my next thought. If they didn't have something against the bull, then maybe someone has a problem with me. I piss off a lot of people. I don't mean to. But if they were going after me and wanted to hurt me, they'd take out Sverre."

"Why?" Reba asked as she took a big scoop of potato salad and put it on her plate.

"He's our pride and joy. He's never been ridden eight seconds. Vidar's a tough son of a bitch, but Sverre is the bull to beat."

"Maybe it was a one-time thing or a freak accident," Reba said, hoping it was true. She pulled out an elote-seasoned corn on the cob. It was coated with butter and cojita cheese and a dusting of breadcrumbs. She squeezed some lime juice on it and dug in. Between the barbecue sauce and that, she was a mess. But she didn't care.

"This is amazing," she said once she swallowed. "Where did you get this?"

"A buddy of mine runs a food truck. He hooks me up when we're at the same event."

They made short work of the chicken and barbecue sauce was everywhere. Bringing over some damp paper towels, Reba sat back down and started cleaning up. Shane helped and stacked the plates and silverware into the RV's small dishwasher. Then he sat down on the floor and let the kittens crawl all over him.

"Since you brought over dinner, how about I treat for dessert? Do you feel like a churro and some ice cream?"

"Hell yeah," Shane said, smiling up at her. Huginn and

Muninn were tackling each other, tumbling around. Hildr was stalking a bug, and Sigrun was curled up in Shane's lap, asleep.

"Holliday Row is playing tonight on stage three in the arena. I know you're probably sick of the rodeo by now, but since we're both technically off work, I figured we could indulge in some fried deliciousness and listen to music."

"Let's go," he said, putting Sigrun back into the padded carrier.

"Round up the kittens and I'll be right back." Reba darted into the bathroom and made sure she didn't have any barbecue sauce on her chin and that there wasn't anything in her teeth. She swiped on a quick dusting of makeup and a soft lip gloss. After putting a brush through her hair, she spritzed on some light perfume.

She was never going to be as flashy as Dolly or as dynamic as LeAnn, but Reba knew that she could hold her own in a conversation. She worried that Shane might want more of a buxom sexy chick, but then again, he was here and not with a buckle bunny so maybe his wild reputation was going to remain in the past.

"All set," Reba said, coming out of the bathroom.

"The kittens have been secured."

Grabbing a jean jacket, she gestured for him to go outside before her. Locking up, Reba smiled up at the sky. "Beautiful night."

"It is now," he said, offering his arm.

She took it and they strolled back to the main section of the rodeo arena. Reba was glad that the UPRC had a separate entrance. They both flashed their badges at the security guard and were let in without having to wait too long in line.

"Have you heard Holliday Row before?" Reba asked.

"Yeah, I like them. They've got a good sound."

"I've been a fan of theirs for years. They got their start at the local rodeos near us," she said.

"I used to stick around after the bull-riding events and listen to them before going out to the bars." Shane shook his head. "I'm pretty sure I survived on coffee, whiskey, and no sleep while I was on the circuit."

"Sleep is overrated."

They had to pass by the stands where the bull-riding event was taking place. Beside her, Shane seemed lost in thought. She could see the wistful expression on his face and couldn't help but wonder what was going through his mind.

"Are you okay?" she asked softly, reaching out to touch his hand.

Shane turned to her, forcing a smile. "Yeah, I'm fine," he said. "Just brings back memories, you know?"

"You must miss it a lot."

"Some days more than others."

"What do you miss the most?" Reba wondered if it was the girls or the adrenaline rush of riding the bulls.

"I miss making a quick buck for doing something I loved."

That surprised her.

"Don't get me wrong, the ranch makes decent money. But it's more of a team effort these days and it takes a while to see the return on our investment."

"And then sometimes the rodeo changes all the rules," she said, referring to the UPRC's new proposed contract with the breeders.

"Exactly. Life was easier back then. I had a good time going from rodeo to rodeo."

"Fast times and sowing wild oats?"

"Yeah," he said. "I feel all adult now, having to get up at an ungodly hour and put in some hard work on the ranch when I'm not at a rodeo babysitting bulls."

"Adulting sucks," Reba said.

"It does indeed. Still, I think I'm getting used to it. Although, I want one last ride to go out in a blaze of glory."

"Why don't you?"

He looked down at the ground and shook his head. "I could fuck up my leg even worse than it is now. It's not worth it for eight seconds of glory."

She squinted at him. "Why don't I believe you?"

"Because you're a smart woman. I figure if I keep telling myself that, it'll sink in and I'll start believing it. Fake it, until you make it."

"Do you want to watch the final rides?" she asked.

"Nope," he said. "I'd rather get a good spot up front to listen to the band."

"But first," Reba said. "Ice cream and churros."

"Naturally."

They shared a big churro, but had their own ice cream. Shane was a purist ordering a dish of two scoops of vanilla. Reba wanted to walk on the wild side a bit and ordered the brown sugar bourbon ice cream.

She closed her eyes in bliss. "You've got to try this."

But when she opened her eyes, Shane was looking at her rather hungrily. She nearly dropped her bowl. And when he tasted a sample of the ice cream off her spoon, Reba felt a rush of heat.

By the time they finished and disposed of their dessert, the band came on stage and started their first song.

"Want to dance?" Shane asked.

"You bet I do." Reba slipped into Shane's arms and even though there wasn't a lot of room, they managed to two-step without bumping into anyone else.

It was easy to dance with him. He was strong and graceful. Reba couldn't help leaning into him and resting her head on his chest when the band played one of their slower songs.

Her phone started buzzing like crazy, but Reba didn't want to answer it. She was off duty if it was a vet call, and her sisters were around if it was family-related. Although, as they twirled as the music became livelier, Reba had a bad thought that maybe LeAnn had gotten hurt.

After the song ended, she pulled her phone out of her back pocket and checked it. There were a bunch of missed calls throughout the day, but no one had left her a voicemail message and she didn't recognize any of the numbers. The most recent notifications came from one number. They called five times in the past hour. "I should see who this is," Reba said apologetically.

"I'll go with you," Shane said, following her away from the band.

She walked toward the veterinarian's compound out of

habit and when she felt she could hear over the crowd and the band, she called the number.

"Reba, is that you?"

"Yes. Who's this?"

"My name is Keith. We met the other day."

Keith Kilgore. Dr. Kilgore's nephew. Reba made a face. "What can I do for you?"

"What are you doing tonight?"

"I'm sorry." *Ugh, why did she apologize?* "I've got plans and I need to get back to them. Is there something you needed?"

"Yeah, let's meet for lunch tomorrow."

"No," Reba said, not elaborating.

"No?"

Just like his uncle. Apparently, Keith wasn't used to hearing that word either. She searched her feelings and realized that facing down another Kilgore didn't fill her with dread.

"Why not?" he asked.

Reba didn't elaborate. She didn't owe anyone an explanation. Surely not an entitled bull rider who thought he could snap his fingers and she would jump.

She wondered if she would be this brave if it was his uncle calling. Reba gave Shane a thoughtful look and realized that Dr. Kilgore was slowly losing his power over her. Part of it was the distance she had from the situation and, thankfully, from him. But part of it was making sure that she didn't sit with the memories anymore and was now reaching out for better memories. Shane was that better memory.

In the awkward silence, Keith stammered, "I-I've got a job offer for you."

"Not interested," she said and hung up on him. She turned to Shane. "I'm not usually that rude."

"Who was it?"

"Keith Kilgore, about a job opportunity."

Shane snorted. "I think you were very polite. I would have told him to fuck off."

"The night's still young," she said. It thrilled her to think that she'd one day have the nerve to say that to Keith's uncle. "Now, where were we?" Reba stepped back into Shane's arms. There was still music to dance to.

Chapter Eight

Shane

H E COULDN'T REMEMBER the last time being with a woman felt so natural. They danced for the entire set and, when the band finished up their last encore, Shane didn't want the night to end just yet. "Do you want to see what kind of trouble we can get into?"

"What kind of trouble?" she asked. Reba had a blush on her pretty face, but she hadn't moved very far away from him, even though they had stopped dancing. He kept his arm around her as they took a long stroll toward the back area where the bulls were hunkered down for the night. "I swear I'm not going to put you to work. But I need to check on my animals and I figure while we're there, we can ask the guys where they're going tonight and maybe tag along."

"All right," Reba said after a slight pause. "I'm not much of a party girl, though."

"We don't have to stay out long. We both have a busy day tomorrow."

She nodded.

The back area was still bustling with activity and the

energy level was high. Shane remembered the endorphin rush after a successful event and the promise of a wild night ahead. He checked in with Pat to make sure everything was going smoothly with settling the bulls down for the evening. There were two more events tomorrow, and the bulls needed to have a good night's rest as well as enough food and water. He looked all of them over carefully, but no one seemed to have been whipped or riled up.

"Which one is Sverre?" Reba asked.

Shane pointed.

"He looks like he's got an attitude."

"Believe me, he does. He's sexy and he knows it."

"So, he's a big hit with all the ladies?"

"He will be once the season is over, especially if he can keep his undefeated record." Shane shrugged. "Maybe even if he doesn't."

"Hey, Doc," Taylor Keating said, walking up to them, smiling broadly at Reba. Shane resisted the urge to sling an arm around her and pull her close. He normally wasn't a jealous type of guy.

"I tried calling earlier," Taylor said. "But I guess you were busy."

Shane frowned, wondering why Taylor would be calling Reba. How did he even have her number? Crossing his arms over his chest, he glared at his friend's son. Taylor was oblivious, though. He hadn't thought Reba was the type to like pretty bull riders, but women were a mystery to him most days.

And then Reba cleared up the matter. "I'm sorry. It was a busy day and I've been screening my calls." She pulled out her phone and asked, "Which number is yours?"

Taylor rattled off his digits and Reba typed his name into her phone. "Now I'll know when it's you calling, instead of someone trying to sell me car insurance or something."

"Great," Taylor said. "I wanted to let you know that Dale seems be doing a lot better."

"I'm glad to hear it. I'll take a look at her first thing tomorrow morning."

There was a pause as Taylor shifted his weight and looked like he was fighting himself into asking for something.

"Unless you would like me to look at her right now?" Reba shot a worried glance at Shane, but Shane just shrugged. Now that he knew it was business and not pleasure that caused Taylor to come over here, they had all night as far as he was concerned.

"If you wouldn't mind looking at her tonight," Taylor said. "I'll sleep a lot easier."

With another look at Shane, who nodded his affirmation, Reba said, "Sure. Let's go."

Shane followed behind them as Reba lectured Taylor about the changes in Dale's diet and exercise. As they got closer to the barn where Dale was, however, he noticed a bunch of bull riders gathered around another one who was causing a bit of a ruckus.

"What's going on there?" Shane asked, gesturing with his chin.

"That's just Mick," Taylor said.

"Is he still pissing and moaning about the wreck he

took last season?" Shane asked.

"Yeah, he says it's the end of the world."

"Oh, for Christ sakes," Shane said. "I'm going to set that boy right." Had Mick gotten stomped on by a bull. Yes. Had he had a concussion? Yes. Did he break his leg in two places? Yes. Mick also had the best treatment that money could buy. And now Mick only walked with a slight limp. Unlike Shane, whose ankle had snapped so badly the back of his shin bone also broke off. He had been an orthopedic surgeon's nightmare. If Shane wasn't out there bitching about the rodeo, there was no reason for Mick to do it either. Mick, at least, could get back on a bull and work a season. He should just shut the fuck up instead of pulling the *woe is me* card.

"Let it go," Reba said with a hand on his arm.

"What? Why?"

"Because he's just looking for attention. If you give him a fight or something that can be put on social media, it just makes him more popular. If you ignore it, eventually people will lose interest."

"I don't know about that," Taylor said. "He's pretty much been a loudmouth for the last year and a half. People like to hear him complain. It gets them riled up and they tend to do things like protest the way animals are being treated."

"Our animals get the very best of care," Reba said, affronted.

"See," Shane said. "It eats at you, doesn't it?"

"Hmm," Reba said. "Well maybe we can compromise a bit. We can let it go, but that doesn't mean the UPRC has to." Reba pulled out her phone and called someone.

"Hi, Dolly?" Reba said. "Do you know bull rider named Mick?"

Shane didn't need to be near the phone to hear Dolly's loud response of "Oh, that asshole? What the hell is he been up to now?"

"He's down by the horse barn with a crowd of people and it looks like he's making a case that the UPRC doesn't take care of their riders or their animals."

"I'll be right there," Dolly said. "Do not engage. This shit ends tonight."

Reba blinked at her phone before slipping it into her pocket. "I know you'd rather handle it," she said to Shane. "But trust me, Dolly knows what to do in these situations."

"You've got a lot of faith in your sister," he said.

"Have you ever seen her in action?" Reba asked.

Shane shook his head. "Nope."

"I wouldn't cross her," Taylor said. "And I run around the arena and grab angry bulls by the horns."

Shane took that under advisement. With one last glare at Mick, he followed Reba and Taylor into the barn. He made himself useful around the stable while Reba treated Taylor's horse, Dale.

Taylor looked a little green around the gills when Reba started her examination. He moved quickly away and joined Shane tidying up the stalls and making sure that all the horses had the correct amount of food and water. It wasn't their job to do it, but all the cowboys looked after each other's horses. It was like an unnamed rule in the UPRC. That was why when Vidar had gotten whipped it was such a betrayal of that unspoken code.

"How did you do today?" Shane asked.

Taylor made a face. "I didn't come in last. But I'm not going to compete tomorrow. My scores weren't high enough."

"You'll get better. Just keep practicing."

"Yeah," he said. "At least I wasn't last. Nash Weaver is always last."

"Who the hell is Nash Weaver?"

"Good question. None of the guys know."

"What do you mean none of the guys know? Everybody knows everybody."

"It's true. None of the bull riders have ever heard of him before this season. Same with the bronc busters, the bulldoggers and certainly not the bullfighters."

"So he just appeared one day?"

"That's it exactly. He's got a bunch of scores that put him in this league, but nobody remembers ever seeing him ride before this year. Between you and me, he sucks."

"Maybe he's somebody's favorite nephew or something. One of the bigwig's kids."

"That must be it. Don't get me wrong, I'm happy that he keeps pushing me up in rank, but I worked hard to get in this league. It kind of chaps my ass that he gets a free ticket without ever having competed professionally before."

"Life is not fair like that, kid," Shane said. "At least you don't have to worry about him stealing the prize money."

"I guess that's something," Taylor said glumly.

"So where are all the bull riders going to party tonight?" Shane asked, trying to change the subject because it looked like Taylor was getting into a funk.

"They're going to hit the Pegasus bar down on Main Street. There was talk about going to a strip show, and some of the guys are probably going to peel off after a few beers. But the Pegasus has a pool tournament and a karaoke contest going on tonight, so that's where the majority of us are to hang out. Are you going to come out?"

"I might," he said.

"Do you think I should ask the doc if she wants to go?" Taylor asked.

"Why? Are you interested in her?" Shane felt his scowl come back and he crossed his arms over his chest again.

"Not especially," Taylor said.

"Good."

"Why is that good?" The light seemed to dawn on Taylor after a second of trying to interpret Shane's glare. "Oh. Oh. *Oh.*" Taylor drew out the last *oh* several syllables.

"Keep your trap shut about it," Shane growled.

"I won't even tell my father."

"Good, because if you tell your father, you might as well take out a billboard."

"I would defend my father's honor," Taylor said. "But that's the God's honest truth."

"Maybe we'll see you there tonight."

"You should. I owe the doc a beer."

Reba wrapped up the examination and cleaned up. She gave Taylor some final instructions and then walked back over to Shane.

"I'm sorry about that," she said.

"That's all right. If it was my horse, I would want you to do the same thing."

"So, you're not mad that I interrupted our date by pressing on a horse's tummy to make it fart?" she asked.

"Not at all. How do you feel about shooting a game of pool and singing, 'My Achy Breaky Heart'?"

"At the same time?" Reba asked. "Because I'm not that talented."

"Taylor tells me that there's a bar called the Pegasus that's having both events tonight. Are you interested in continuing our date down there?"

"We could," Reba said hesitantly. "Or we could go back to the Winnebago and extend our date to breakfast."

Her words caught him off guard, causing his heart to skip a beat. Had he heard that correctly? He usually wasn't this lucky with beautiful women.

"Unless you think this is going too fast," she said.

"I like fast," he said, his mind racing with possibilities. "Kissing you has been on my mind all day," he admitted, his hand reaching for hers.

Her touch sent a jolt of electricity through him, making him feel alive and energized.

"Same," she said softly, her eyes meeting his.

Shane squeezed her hand, anticipation washing over him. "I feel I need to warn you. I'm not a romantic guy. If you're looking for roses and chocolates, I'm not the one."

Reba nodded slowly. Her fingers went to the buttons on her shirt. He watched greedily as she unbuttoned two, giving him a tantalizing look at her cleavage. "As long as we're giving out warnings, I'll let you know that I'm not one of those girly girls who'll get bent out of shape if you muss my lipstick or track dirt on the floor. But I'd be remiss if I didn't remind you that castrating a bull is all in a day's work to me. So you may want to rethink this, if you think you can play fast and hard with my emotions."

He winced at the image. "I'm not that kind of guy either."

"Good. Let's go back to my place and get to know each other a little better."

"Yes, ma'am," Shane said.

Reba

DID SHE HAVE the jitters? Sure. But she also wanted to feel Shane's arms around her. It had been a long time since she felt comfortable enough with a man to allow him into the RV, not to mention her bed. But he made her feel safe and his good looks flustered her, had since the first time she saw him.

And she needed to kiss him more than she needed to breathe. Taking his hand, they walked fast back to the Winnebago. Once they were inside, she led him to the back of the RV where her bedroom was. It was cramped having him in there with her, but cozy. Easing into the back corner, she kicked off her shoes and lay down, propping herself up on her elbow.

Shane sat down on the corner of the bed and took off his boots before matching her pose on the other pillow.

"It's been a while," Reba said, her voice barely above a whisper.

"We don't have to take this any farther than you want it to go."

His words soothed her, but she wanted more than a few kisses. But first, she was going to start with one. Leaning in, she brushed her lips against his, felt him smile against her mouth. Shane cupped her cheek and deepened the kiss until her toes curled. Reba hooked her calf over his and snuggled in close to him. He smelled good, like the outdoors and fresh, clean hay. This was what she wanted. This was what she had been missing out on.

They kissed for long moments, inching closer until they were in each other's arms. It felt so good to be held and kissed like she was the last woman on earth. Shane's kisses were thrilling, but she wanted more. After tugging his shirt loose from his pants, Reba pulled it over his head. While he worked at the buttons on her shirt, she traced the hard muscles of his arms and chest.

"What happened here?" she asked, huskily as she traced a thick scar on his side.

"Got gored by one of our bulls," he said, his breathing heavy. Shane kissed her shoulder as he peeled her shirt off her. "I should have waited until he got tipped before riding him, but I thought I was invincible. The bull had other ideas. One of the many dumb things I did when I was younger."

He made short work of her bra and took her breasts in

his hands. Shane rubbed his thumbs over her nipples before taking each one in his mouth. Reba's head went back and she cried out in the sudden shock of pleasure. He ran his tongue over them, licking and then sucking on them until she was squirming and panting.

"Damn," she said. "That feels so good."

"Gorgeous," he said in between worshiping the hardened peaks.

Her hands fumbled with his belt, trying to unfasten it. Shane didn't give up an inch though, just caught her tighter to him and kept at her breasts until she was a quivering mass of need.

"Shane." She gasped just before his mouth captured hers again.

Her sensitive breasts crushed against the wiry hairs of his chest. Reba ran her hands up and down his muscled back, desperate for more of him. When he was done kissing her senseless, he moved to the sweet spot at the juncture of her neck and shoulder. Reba saw stars. She had to hold on to his shoulders to keep from spinning away in sweet passion. She was dimly aware of him unfastening her jeans and easing them off her hips.

Kissing down her chest, to her belly, Shane pulled her jeans and underwear down her legs and tossed them on the floor.

"You're wearing too many clothes," Reba protested half-heartedly.

"I just need to do something first," he said, settling between her thighs.

"What's that?" she asked.

"Make you come." Then he buried his face between her thighs while wrapping his arms around her hips.

Reba gripped the sheets as all the air left her body in a shocked, pleasured gasp. His tongue was magic as it danced inside her, hitting every erogenous zone she had. The wet sound of him lapping up her arousal brought her closer to the edge with each stroke. Tingles of erotic pleasure shot up and down her body. Her hips twitched and rolled as Shane went faster.

Her release shuddered through her and Reba called out his name. He licked her a few more times and she jostled and gasped as her frazzled nerve endings pulsed.

"Now, I'll get rid of these."

She could only watch in a haze of desire as he chucked off his jeans. Greedily, she gazed at his hardness and her fingers ached to stroke him.

"Come here," she breathed.

Reaching into his pocket, he came out with a foil packet.

"I'll just be a second," he said, and he tore it open and rolled it down on his erection. Then his body covered hers. Her legs wrapped around his hips and he drove deep inside her. Her fingernails dug into his shoulders as his lips came down on hers. He plundered her mouth as his body rocked into hers with long, hard strokes.

Arching into each thrust, Reba moaned against his kisses. This felt too good. Too perfect. He slid in and out of her in a rhythm that built up the anticipation until she was frenzied again. Clamping down on him, she loved the sweet friction against her sensitive folds.

"Oh, sweetheart," Shane moaned, his body shaking.

"Yes," Reba cried, her orgasm cresting into a wave of sweet seduction that had her eyes crossing.

"Just like that, darlin'," he said, before following her with a strained groan.

Gathering her up into his arms, he rolled over on his back so she sprawled across him.

"Just like that." She sighed and kissed him. She felt a little more of the hold Dr. Kilgore had in her nightmares slip away. Putting the past where it belonged was going to be a lot of fun, and she was looking forward to more days and nights of good times like this.

Chapter Nine

Shane

THE NEXT MORNING Shane was a little disoriented. His body recognized a warm soft woman next to him. That confused him because it had been long time since that had happened. Realization hit him about the time his phone rang, waking both him and Reba up a good half hour before their alarm was supposed to have gone off.

"Shit," he said. "Sorry."

Reba muttered and rolled over.

He found his underwear and pants and carried them out into the other room so that he wouldn't disturb Reba with his phone call. Of course, the Winnebago was small enough that she could probably hear him anyway. "Hello," he snapped.

"Mr. Calland, this is Jackson Blevins of the UPRC."

"Yeah?" Shane had a vague idea that this was someone relatively important in the organization, but it wasn't the usual person he spoke with. After pulling on his pants, he decided that since he was up, he might as well feed the kittens. "What can I do for you?"

"I'm not sure if you've heard, but the UPRC is going to

be doing things a little bit differently from now on concerning how we get our animal stock."

Here it comes, Shane thought. *Thank you, but no thank you. We'll see you when we see you.* He fought to keep a lid on his temper, but it just wasn't fair. Everyone knew that the new guy in was the first one to go. But they'd worked so hard to get to this level. It really pissed him off that his bulls wouldn't get the chance to compete in this league. He wondered if that would change things between him and Reba, but then he shook himself out of that. Reba wasn't Abigail. He shouldn't have to remind himself about that, not after all these years.

"We would like to offer you an invitation to be one of the three bull breeders to provide stock for our rodeos for the next five years."

"Five years," Shane said, shock warring with disbelief that they had been chosen to be one of the three. The cynical part of him wondered how many other people turned the offer down before they got to the Viking Ranch's name on their list.

"Yes," Blevins said. "It's an exclusive contract; however, I think that you'll find it a lucrative one."

"And what happens at the end of five years?"

"We'll negotiate another contract for another set period of time."

It sounded fair to him. "How much are we talking about for the exclusive right?"

Blevins named a figure that wasn't out of the question.

"I have to speak to my family about this, but I think we can come to an arrangement." The kittens mewed loudly, and Shane resisted the urge to shush them. Not only did he not want Blevins to hear them, but he also didn't want to have them wake Reba up with their caterwauling. He quickly squeezed the tube of kitten food into four separate blobs on the plastic mat that Reba had laid out. The kittens quieted down as they slurped up the goo.

"Good," Blevins said. "I'll have our legal department email over the paperwork."

"I'll have an answer to you after the Fort Worth rodeo next week," Shane said.

That would mean he would have to fly home to Montana to talk about this with his father and brother face-to-face. He'd have to make arrangements with Pat to trailer the bulls by himself to the next rodeo.

He sat down after getting the kittens water and ran his fingers down their soft little backs and curled around each of their little tails. He was getting attached to them. Just like he was getting attached to Reba. It hadn't taken long.

REBA CAME OUT of the bedroom wearing his shirt. "Is everything all right?" she asked, moving over by him to the kitchen area to make a pot of coffee.

"More than all right. You look gorgeous."

He came up behind her and nuzzled her neck. She leaned back into his chest. "I had a great time last night."

"Me, too." Sliding his hand up her shirt, he cupped her breast. "Are you wearing anything underneath that?"

"Why don't you find out?"

Shane didn't need to be asked twice. Reaching around their bodies, he slid his fingers between her parted thighs. She was wet for him.

"Oh, sweetheart," he moaned. Sliding through her slick folds, he fingered her gently with one hand, while rolling her nipple with his other.

Reba tilted her head back to kiss him. Her tongue teased him and he flicked faster.

"Mmm." She gasped.

"Are you going to come for me, sweetheart?"

"Oh yeah."

Her little sighs were driving him wild. She trembled against him and cried out when he ground against her. Shane was about to burst out of his jeans. Her thighs clamped around him as she shook.

"Shane," she said. Reaching into the pocket of his shirt, she pulled out one of the condoms they had left over from last night.

"Fuck yeah," he said, ripping the foil wrapper off. He yanked down his pants and slid the condom on over his ready cock. Flipping up the tail of his shirt, Shane admired the soft globes of her ass. "Bend over, sweetheart."

Reba gripped the edge of the counter and wiggled her ass suggestively at him. He pulled her hips to him and slid inside her soaking wet heat. He went in deep and held her hips to him. She was tight and anxious as she tried to get him to move.

"In a minute, darlin'. I'm enjoying how damned good you feel." He kissed her neck, grazing it with his teeth.

"Please, Shane," she breathed, bucking against him.

"I like hearing you say my name when I'm deep inside you." He rocked into her with long languid strokes.

"Yes," Reba cried out, pushing back against him.

It was suddenly too much for him. Losing control, he took her fast and hard. Her body was so sweet, he could get lost in the taste and feel of her. He wanted this every morning, every night. He had never felt this way about a woman before. He was in over his head, but he was loving every minute of it.

Reba tightened around him. "Oh God," she said. "Shane."

He felt her come all around him. His vision grew dim as lightning seemed to go off in his brain. Reba squeaked with each panting breath and then went limp. He couldn't believe the pleasure he felt when she came apart in his arms and sagged against him. He was close behind her and with a few more glorious thrusts, he followed her over the edge into bliss.

"You're amazing," he said.

"I'm only sorry there's not enough room for two in my shower," she said, turning around and kissing him.

They could have kissed all day, but Reba's second alarm went off. "Shit," she said. "I've got to get ready."

"Go ahead. I'll make coffee and breakfast."

"Careful," she said and gave him another deep kiss. "I could get used to this."

"I'm counting on it," he said, filling up the coffee pot with water.

In the small freezer, he found microwave sausages. In the little refrigerator, there was a loaf of bread and eggs. He scrambled the eggs up while the toaster did its thing. He timed it perfectly, so everything was ready by the time Reba got out of the shower.

"I'm going to jump in for a quick one."

"A real quick one because there's not much hot water left."

He handed her a plate of food and went into the bathroom to clean up. After getting washed and dressed, he was more than ready for a cup of coffee. Reba was playing with the kittens when he came back into the kitchen.

"Who was that on the phone before?" she asked, getting up to pour him a cup of coffee.

He sliced up the sausage and added it to the scrambled eggs he had made in between two slices of bread. "Jackson Blevins."

"The CEO of the UPRC?

"Huh, that make sense." He explained to her about the offer. "I'm still in shock."

"Why? Your animals are well taken care of and excellent athletes. Sverre, in particular, is going to be a bull to beat. So, it makes perfect sense that the Viking Ranch was one of the choices."

"I've got to fly home and talk about the offer with my father and my brother. I was wondering, would you like to come home with me?"

"I've always liked Montana," she said. "We never had a chance to stay very long when we were there because LeAnn was only in town for the rodeo, and then it was on to the next one before we had a chance to see more of the state."

"I can't be gone too long. I've got to be at Fort Worth next week."

"Me, too," she said.

"Can you get away tomorrow?"

Reba thought about it. "I think so. I'll have to check and see if Dolly can drive the Winnebago to Fort Worth for me. I'd love to see the Viking Ranch. I'll be honest, though, I'm a little nervous about meeting your family. Do you always bring home strange women?"

"You'd be the first that I wasn't already married to." He picked up one of the kittens. "I need to be honest, too. I have to admit there is an ulterior motive to me asking you to come with me."

"What's that?" she asked suspiciously.

"I want to take the kittens home with me."

Reba clasped her hand over her mouth, her eyes wide with shock and delight.

"We're going to have to get another carrier, but I think if we fit two in one carrier and two in the other, the airline will let them fly with us in the cabin."

Reba ran around the small table and flung her arms around his neck. "I can't believe it. You're going to adopt all four?"

"I can't very well separate them now, can I?"

"You're the best. The absolute best." She covered his face with kisses. "Of course I'll help bring the kittens home."

Shane would adopt all the kittens she wanted if this was the thanks he got. He captured her mouth and kissed her long and sweet. He'd like nothing better than to drag her back into bed and make love to her all day long. But of course, they were interrupted by another phone call. This time it was Reba's phone.

"Sorry, I've got to get this," she said. "It's my boss, Diane."

Shane wrangled the kittens back into their carrier while Reba finished her call.

"I need to head on over to the 4-H tent. We've got a sick goat." She tossed him her keys. "Can you lock up? If you're free for lunch this afternoon, we can talk more about the flight."

"It's a date," he said.

She hugged him again and hurried out of the Winnebago.

Shane had a full day of work to put in, in between making travel arrangements for himself, Reba, and the kittens. He was able to hire a couple of cowboys to help Pat get the bulls on the trailer tomorrow while he and Reba took the flight out to Montana.

"I hate to do this to you, Pat," Shane said. "But I want to get a jump on this with Dad and Rick."

"I understand," Pat said. "Rick will be on board, but Bill is going to give you a hard time about it, just because he doesn't like change."

"Ain't that the truth. But I'll make him see reason." Shane was also hoping that having Reba there would put his father on his best behavior.

Around lunchtime, he walked over to the veterinarian's trailer, eager to see Reba.

"I don't have time for a sit-down meal or anything like

that," she said. "But if you want to grab a sandwich and are willing to eat while we walk, I'd love to spend some time with you."

"Sounds good to me." Being with Reba was easy.

"How do you feel about a brisket sandwich and some fried pickles?" she asked.

"Throw in some fried Oreos and you got yourself a deal."

"I know just the place," she said.

While they waited in line for the sandwiches, Shane called up the flight information on his phone. "Would you be able to fly out with me first thing tomorrow morning?"

"Yes. Dolly was okay with driving the RV to Fort Worth for me. Luckily, she was going there anyway. I just have to drop off her car at the rental place tonight. I was able to get Victor Lance—he's one of the other vets on staff—to take over my on-call hours tomorrow. It means I'll be doing double duty in Fort Worth, but that's not a big deal."

"I'm sorry about that. I'd understand, since it's so last minute, if you decided not to come with me. I'll manage the kittens somehow."

"No." Reba shook her head. "Nothing to be sorry about. You're giving four little angel kittens a permanent home. It's the least I could do. And I probably will just be hanging around the RV anyway while I'm on call."

"Maybe you and I can hang around together in Fort Worth while you're on call—if that's allowed?"

"I'm sure it'll be fine. It's not like when I'm actively doing examinations. But you never know what comes when you're on call. Anything could happen and nothing could happen." She shrugged.

"I just really enjoy spending time with you," Shane said.

"Yeah?" She smiled up at him, and it felt like the sun came out from behind the clouds. "I didn't think I was your type."

"I have a type?"

Reba waved her hand vaguely at the other people around them. "I'm not your typical rodeo queen."

"No," he said. "You're better."

"You're dangerous," she said.

"Why am I dangerous?"

"Because you're sexy and charming."

Shane barked out a laugh. "I've never been called charming before."

After they got their sandwiches, they walked back to the vet trailer. Reba had a list of things she needed to do, but she let him drive the golf cart while she finished her lunch.

"I'm booking the flights now," he said. "Do you need me to give you a ride back from the car rental place tonight?"

"No. LeAnn's coming with me."

"Okay. What time will you be ready tomorrow morning?" he asked.

"That depends on when we wake up." She leaned over and gave him a kiss.

Yeah, he could definitely get used to this.

"I gotta get back to work. Sorry to strand you, but I

need the golf cart."

"Not a problem. I need to work off the fried Oreos anyway."

The rodeo was in full swing today. Saturday was their busiest day. There were several events going on at once. A ton of families were out and about, and Shane was happy to see a lot of the youth organizations getting involved. There was everything from mutton busting where elementary and middle-school-age children rode sheep, to 4-H events that focused on taking care of animals and showing the high schoolers how to make a profit from selling their stock at auction. That was how he had started out.

The adult events also drew a large crowd. The women's bronc busting was just as exciting as the men's event. It had had a rough and rocky start a few years ago, but now it was mainstream. Change was good. Shane would just have to convince his father that being exclusive to the UPRC was the right thing to do for their business. Although, a small voice in the back of his head wondered if that was really the case.

It was a risk to put all your eggs, or this case your bulls, in one basket. But there wasn't any denying that the UPRC was one of the biggest rodeo outfits in the world. Getting in now could only help the Viking Ranch. And if the ranch made bank with this new contract, then maybe Shane's father would finally retire. Maybe if they made a shit-ton of cash, he could buy himself a fishing boat down in Florida and spend his days trying to catch mermaids or marlins.

When Shane got back to the bull-riding area, everybody should have been by the front where the bulls were being led into the chutes or waiting in the holding pens for the next rider. There shouldn't have been anyone in this back area, which is why he was surprised to see Taylor Keating in the same pen as his bulls.

"What the hell you doing?" Shane asked. "You know you're not supposed to be in there."

Taylor raised up his hands as two of Shane's bulls snorted and started to menace the young man. "Don't get them all riled up. I'm trying to get them used to me." Taylor slowly backed away, making sure not to make any sudden moves that might enrage or excite the bulls.

Once Taylor was back over on the right side of the fence, Shane raised his voice. "It's dangerous for both you and for the bulls to be here. You should have at least had somebody with you."

"I didn't want to get anyone in trouble."

"Then why did you do this?"

"I need something to give me an edge," Taylor said. "I can't practice any more than I have been. I don't have enough time, what with bullfighting and bull riding."

And going out to karaoke and playing pool, Shane thought. He didn't say that aloud because when he was Taylor's age, he had sowed a lot of his own wild oats. "You need to pick one," Shane said instead. "Either you're a bull rider or a bullfighter. Otherwise, you're going to be mediocre at both."

"What you think I should do?"

"That's up to you. Do what you love more."

"I love both," Taylor said. "I love getting paid. I'd make more money bull riding if I could win an event. But bullfighting pays me a steady salary."

"Sounds to me like you've got a tough choice to make," Shane said. "You can quit the sure thing and start practicing more and see if you can succeed, going eight seconds consistently. Or you can do bull riding for fun and keep your steady paycheck."

"That's the gist of it. Although, bull riders get more girls," Taylor said.

"Sometimes quality is better than quantity." That had been a tough lesson for Shane to learn. And he wasn't sure that Taylor would agree with them. But Shane would rather have one night with Reba, than several nights with a woman like his ex-wife Abigail.

"Yeah, the girls don't really see bullfighters as anything other than a glorified rodeo clown."

"The right one will appreciate you for who you are," Shane said, even though he was pretty sure he was wasting his breath.

"Yeah, you got a point."

"Shouldn't you be getting ready to do some bullfighting?" Shane said, remembering that Taylor said his numbers weren't good enough for him to be competing today.

"I'll suit up," Taylor said. "But I'm not on the roster. I had hoped to be riding today."

"Well, you know how Murphy's Law is," Shane said. "Someone will need you somewhere. If you're looking for some extra work, Pat could use a hand with the bulls tomorrow. I'm headed back to Montana for a few days."

"Is everything all right at home?" Taylor asked, concerned.

"Yeah, I just need to talk to my dad and brother about a few things in person."

Taylor got a crafty look in his eye. "Does this have anything to do with an offer?"

Blevins told Shane to keep this hush-hush, and Shane didn't want to jinx anything, or worse start a rumor. For all he knew, his father would put his foot down and demand to keep supplying all of the other rodeos instead of going UPRC's exclusive contract.

Shane just shook his head. "I don't think any of the breeders have been finalized yet." That was safe enough to say. "Now get the hell on out of here. If I catch you back in here again, I'm going to have to report you to security."

"All right," Taylor said. "That's fair."

"But if you do want to get some practice in," Shane said. "Let me know. We might be able to arrange something."

"I appreciate that."

Chapter Ten

Reba

THE KITTENS WERE too tiny for her to risk giving them a sedative for the flight. But luckily, they weren't fretting because they had full bellies. She and Shane made it a point to keep their fingers through the holes of the carriers when they were allowed to have them on their lap after take-off. Although, she had to steady his when he fell asleep.

It was fun to take a last-minute flight to another state. This wasn't something that she got to do very often. Usually when they traveled, she was the driver. And she certainly never had a handsome man sitting next to her—even if this handsome man was snoring his fool head off.

She nibbled on a cookie and watched out the window of the airplane, fretting a little bit about whether the change in cabin pressure would affect the kittens.

"Don't worry, guys," she said. "Once we get you to the Viking Ranch, you'll be at your forever home. There will be lots of food, mice, and people to love you." At least, she hoped so. To be honest, she didn't know how his family had reacted when Shane told them there would be four more mouths to feed. But the Viking Ranch had a stellar reputation and who didn't love kittens, really?

Still, she was a little nervous about meeting his father and brother. Would he introduce her as his girlfriend? Were they even boyfriend and girlfriend? She would like to be. Reba did catch the bouquet at LeAnn's wedding after all. Of course, she had to elbow Dolly in the tit in order to steal it away from her.

Shane woke up about half an hour before landing. He gave her hand a reassuring squeeze. "I can't wait to show you around the ranch," he said.

"I'm looking forward to it, too."

"I've got to warn you, though, my father can be a little abrasive sometimes."

"That's okay," Reba said. "So, can I."

Because they had only carry-ons and the kittens, they deplaned and went right out to grab a rental car.

"I don't suppose you want to stop at a liquor store for a bottle of whiskey to give me a little liquid courage?" she asked.

"Not that you'll need it," he said. "But trust me, there will be a full bar available for you as soon as we get to the house."

They made it to his ranch in record time, but Reba was exhausted. She didn't think she could handle a big family thing right now. But it didn't look like she was going to have a choice. Shane's family was waiting for them on the porch. His mom and dad stood up as they came up the driveway. A pretty woman with red hair and freckles and a younger man who had to be Shane's brother were there, too. The redhead came bounding down the stairs and took one of the cat carriers from Reba. "Are these the kittens? I can't wait to see them."

"Hello to you, too, Lainey," Shane said.

"Right," Lainey said, flustered. "I'm Lainey Evans." She held out her hand to Reba. "I'm a big fan of your sister."

"Hi, I'm Reba Keller." Reba remembered Shane telling her that Lainey was his brother Rick's long-time girlfriend. "LeAnn's something else, isn't she?"

"Are you a bull rider, too?" Shane's father asked.

Reba could see where Shane got his piercing eyes and forbidding scowl from. Shane's mother rolled her eyes behind her husband's back.

"This is *Dr.* Reba Keller," Shane said, emphasizing the word doctor. He handed Lainey the other cat carrier and hugged his mother. "Reba, this is my dad, Bill, and my mother, Mary."

"It's nice to meet you. You have a beautiful home," Reba said.

"My brother, Rick." Shane pointed to a younger version of himself who was standing in the doorway of the house.

"Come inside," Mary said warmly.

"Can I get you guys a beer?" Rick asked, holding the door open for them.

"That would be great," Reba said. She cautiously moved around Bill, who was still glowering at her suspiciously.

Everybody piled into the house. Rick handed her an ice-cold beer and gestured to the large but cozy family room. She gratefully sank into an overstuffed chair and immediately wished she could kick off her boots and close her eyes. Everyone got drinks and sat down as well. Shane's father turned on the TV. Rick reached over and turned the sound down.

"I was watching that," Bill said.

"I'll put on the closed captions." Mary fiddled with a few buttons.

Bill made a face and turned back to scowl at Reba. "So what are you a doctor of?"

"I'm a veterinarian," Reba said.

"You take care of kittens?" He pointed to the four little ones that Lainey had freed from their carriers. She and Mary had sat on the floor and were feeding them from the snack tubes. The kittens were mewing and pawing in an adorable manner.

"I mostly do large farm animals."

It was like the sun suddenly came out. "Oh really?" Bill said, now all smiles.

"Here we go," Shane said.

"Before we start in on that…" Mary said. "You mentioned that you had some important news to tell us." She looked from Reba to Shane. "Isn't this rather sudden?"

Reba choked on her beer.

"No, it's not like that," Shane said, shooting Reba an apologetic look. "Reba agreed to come with me to help with the kittens."

"So you're not pregnant or getting married?" Mary asked, disappointment flashing over her face.

Reba put the beer bottle down on the coaster on the

table before she had an accident.

"No," Reba said.

"Mom, really." Shane sighed. "I wanted to wait until tomorrow morning when we were all rested, but I hadn't realized you were playing guessing games."

Lainey shrugged. "I thought it might be you were getting back into bull riding."

Shane shot his brother an incredulous look. Where was all this coming from?

"I kept my mouth shut," Rick said.

"You know what this is all about?" Lainey looked hurt and betrayed.

"You're not getting back into bull riding, are you, son?" Mary asked.

"Fu—" Shane corrected himself. "Of course not. What I wanted to discuss in person has to do with the UPRC's new rules for the bull breeders that are providing livestock."

"What bullshit hoops do we have to jump through now?" Bill asked.

"Starting next season, they're only going to be using three bull breeders."

Mary slumped and put her head in her hands. "We worked so hard to get in there. Why did they have to move the goal post?"

"Who gives a shit?" Bill said. "We don't need them anyway."

"Actually, they want us to be one of three breeders."

Mary looked up in shock. "Really?"

"What's the catch?" Bill said.

"The catch is we have to be exclusive to them for five

years."

Bill was already shaking his head.

"Are they paying for the privilege?" Mary asked.

Shane nodded. "They sent me over the terms and contract via email. I'll send it to you guys to review."

"I don't want to read on the tiny screen. Go print it out," Mary said.

"Read it over," Shane said, getting up. "We can discuss it tomorrow. Reba and I have had a full day and we need to get some sleep. Tomorrow morning, I want to take her out around the ranch. Let's plan on discussing what we're going to do over dinner."

"Fine," Bill said. "But I don't think I like this deal."

"Lainey, can you show Reba to the guest room. I want to talk to Shane for a bit," Mary said.

"Sure, I'd be glad to." Lainey gently dumped one of the kittens into Mary's lap and got up.

Reba hoped Shane could convince his parents.

"I think this would be good for ranch," Shane said.

Reba gave a small smile of encouragement to Shane. Picking up her overnight bag, she followed Lainey up the stairs. The guest bedroom looked like something out of a cozy retreat. There was a large king-size bed covered with an antique wedding-ring quilt.

"How long have you been dating Shane?" Lainey asked.

Good question. "Not too long."

"Well, I hope you're in it for the long run," Lainey said sadly. "I've been dating Rick since high school." She showed Reba the back of her left hand. "No ring yet. And not one in sight, either."

"It's way too early for that for us," Reba said. "Shane and I are just enjoying each other's company."

"That's nice." Lainey showed her the bathroom that was attached to the bedroom and handed her a set of fluffy blue towels. "Sometimes, I forget what that's like. Especially when you live in a small town like this and every day someone asks you: so when are you two ever getting married?"

"I can see how that would be uncomfortable." They talked about the care of the kittens, while Reba unpacked. By the time she was finished, Reba was satisfied that Lainey would check in on the kittens daily, and make sure they were well taken care of.

"I'm here for several hours every day anyway. And I love cats, so this is a real treat. I can't believe you got Shane to adopt all four, the big softy."

"He was the one who found them, after all," Reba said. "Or maybe they found him."

"I'll leave you to get settled," Lainey said. She gave Reba her phone number in case she needed anything. "I'll see you at dinner tomorrow."

After she left, Reba took a quick shower and got into her nightgown. She was near dead on her feet. The bed beckoned and she got under the covers. She planned on reading a bit to settle down before going to sleep.

She was surprised at a soft knock on her door about half an hour later. It was Shane.

"Congratulations," he said. "You survived the first round."

"What happens in the next round?" Reba asked, smiling as she put away the book she was reading.

"That's when you dodge my father as he tries to get free veterinarian services on all thousand head of our cattle."

"That's a lot of exams," Reba said.

"I'd avoid him at all costs unless you're with me," he said. "I won't let him be a pest, but if he does catch you alone, be firm and don't be afraid to set boundaries."

"I'll try."

"So, are you tired?" he asked, sitting on the bed next to her.

"Depends on what you had in mind. Jogging? Yes, way too tired. Having more mind-blowing sex? I'm all in."

"Excellent." He reached under the covers and picked her up in his arms.

She gave a little shriek. "Shane, what are you doing?"

"I'm taking you back to my bed, where you're going to sleep all night with me after I lick and kiss every single inch of you."

Reba shivered, her toes curling at his husky words.

"No need to keep it down, either," he said. "My father's deaf as a post and my mother wears headphones so she doesn't have to hear him snore."

"What makes you think I'm going to get loud?"

"Trust me."

He carried her out of the room and down the hall like she weighed nothing. He nudged open a solid onyx door with his foot and then lightly kicked it closed behind him. Shane's bedroom looked like paradise to her. It was three times as big as hers in the RV. Another king-sized bed was in the center of the room. Above the bed was a large skylight through which Reba could see the stars overhead.

"Have I mentioned how beautiful you are?" he asked, gently putting her down. Shane made short work of pulling her soft cotton nightgown over her head. She wasn't wearing anything underneath that.

"Not today," she said, resisting the urge to cover up. She wasn't used to anyone looking at her with such frank admiration.

Reba kissed down his strong muscled chest, sinking to her knees before him. She unbuckled his pants and pushed them down to his ankles. After he stepped out of them and kicked them aside, she gripped his hardness in her hand.

"Now that's a pretty sight," he said huskily.

Cupping his balls, she ran her thumb lightly over them and licked up his shaft. "You taste good," she said and swirled her tongue around him.

He gripped his fingers through her hair and brought her mouth down on him. "Why don't you show me what you can do with that pretty mouth of yours," he said.

Reba drew him slowly in and out of her mouth, dragging her tongue and just a trace of teeth alongside him.

Shane groaned in appreciation and pushed deeper into her throat. She let him control her head as he rocked his hips slowly. She looked up at him, mesmerized by the sweet play of emotion on his face. She liked giving him pleasure like this.

"Maybe I'm the one who's going to get loud," he said, his breath heavy.

Reba increased her efforts, never taking her eyes off him as she pleasured him with her mouth. His muscled ass felt good as she squeezed it.

"Sweetheart." He gasped as she swallowed around him and moaned.

He clenched and lost control, swearing softly and incoherently.

When she finished him, Reba let him slowly out of her mouth with a soft pop and kissed back up his chest.

"That was incredible," he said. Shane laid her down on the bed and spread her legs wide so he could return the favor.

The rasp of his beard on her inner thighs made her aquiver in anticipation. Shane took his time, licking and probing her sensitive spots with his tongue before lapping away at her tiny bud.

Now it was her turn to grip his hair and guide his mouth to where she wanted it. His soft sucking made her eyes cross with pleasure and she felt sweet pressure build up as she moved her hips in time with his mouth on her core.

"Shane," she whispered, every inch of her on fire for him.

Trembling with each pass of his tongue inside her, Reba stared up at the night sky. The stars seemed to twinkle just for them, and she moaned long and loud as the orgasm built up in her and then cascaded over until her back arched and she gripped the bedspread as she shook apart.

Reba was barely aware of Shane putting on a condom. He lay on his back and pulled her on top of him. She teased her breasts in his face while they fumbled to put him inside her. When he slipped in, she sank down hard, gasping at his thickness.

"Come here, sweetheart," he said, taking her breast in his hand to guide her nipple into his mouth.

Reba bounced on him, while he sat up, holding her tight so he could play with her chest and suck hard on her nipples while she rode him. She liked being in control, liked how their bodies contorted so they could give each other maximum pleasure.

Her thrusts became too vigorous for him to hold on and he fell back to the pillows. Shane kept his hands on her hips as she went wild, loving the hard feel of him hitting all the right places. The friction was sweet. Reba was desperate to reach that pinnacle again. She groaned his name, and he cupped her swinging breasts to tease her nipples again.

"Oh," she cried out over and over again. Every plunge of his body into hers was sweet torture and she wanted it harder, deeper, longer.

She shook her hair, arched her back and held on to his shoulders while she rode him. It took more than eight seconds, more than eight minutes, but she was on the ride of her life.

"Coming," Reba shrieked, and Shane grinned.

"Fuck yeah," he said.

Squeezing him, she shuddered and quaked. Her mouth opened in a startled cry as the pleasure rushed through her, shredding any sense of self-control she had. Sagging, Reba let him roll her over until he was on top.

And then it began again. Her ankles hooked behind his back, Reba gripped his strong biceps and kissed him fiercely as he pounded into her. The bed was making a racket and she was glad they wouldn't be overheard because

Shane was taking her to places she had never even imagined of.

She came again as his body relentlessly drilled into her. Moaning into his mouth, she welcomed his returning shout as he shuddered and emptied himself inside her. Shaking and breathing heavily, she still couldn't stop kissing him and another tiny starburst of pleasure thrilled through her as he pulled out.

"I could get used to this," he said, kissing her once more before leaving to go clean up.

"Me, too." She sighed, watching his muscled ass as he went into the bathroom.

Chapter Eleven

Reba

S HANE'S FATHER WAS at the breakfast table waiting for them when they got up the next morning. "So, Reba, how would you like to take a look at the herd today?"

"She's going to ride out with me, Dad." Shane laid a hand on his father's shoulder and gave him a warning squeeze. "She's here on a mini-vacation, not to work as a veterinarian."

"I wasn't about to put her to work," Bill sputtered.

Bullshit. Reba hid her smile behind her coffee cup.

After breakfast, she and Shane headed out to the barn. The ranch had Viking accents all around from the runes engraved on the doorframes to the Nordic artwork and wood carvings around the farm.

The weather was brisk this time of year, so she borrowed a sheepskin jacket from the barn. It smelled like Shane, and it wrapped around her like hug. She saddled up on a sturdy Morgan horse that had a disposition that was neither sweet nor surly. Reba got the impression that the horse couldn't care less if he had a rider on his back or not.

The Viking Ranch was impressive. She enjoyed the

wide-open spaces and the bustling nature of the farm. They spent the day riding around, stopping for a picnic lunch from the basket that Mary had made them this morning.

"Does Lainey spend a lot of time here?" Reba asked when Rick passed by with a wave as he rode through, close by where they were sitting.

"Not as much time as she'd like. She runs a restaurant in town, but she'd rather be a rancher's wife. Unfortunately, Rick is not in a hurry to make that happen."

"I hope he doesn't wait too long," Reba said. "He might lose her. You can't expect a girl like that to wait around forever."

"Yeah, you're preaching to the choir. It's what my father and I have been saying for the past two years now. I don't know why he's hesitating. It's obvious he's crazy about her. And vice versa. I think he's waiting for my father to retire, though."

"Why?"

"With my father in charge, all decisions have to go through him. When he retires, Rick and I will be co-owners. We can get a lot of stuff done that we've been wanting to do. Rick, in particular, wants to take the ranch into the future or at least the twenty-first century. I think once he has the autonomy to do what he wants, he'll feel more settled and settle down."

"What about you?"

"I like the old ways. It's how we've always done it. It's how my great-grandfather built this ranch. It's not that I don't trust new technologies. I'm not an idiot. I can see how much easier machines and computers have made our lives. But on the other hand, the machines can't take the place of human intuition and human sweat and work ethic."

"Yeah, I can see that. But it's getting harder and harder to make ends meet. And if you can save some money off your bottom line by streamlining processes, it's a good idea to at least look into that."

"I know it. And I'm a little bit more reasonable about it than my father is. He just shuts Rick down without explanation, and Rick doesn't want to argue with him unless it's a life-or-death situation. So, the ranch has been floundering in the last couple years because my father's too stubborn to try something new, and my brother's not aggressive enough to force his hand."

"And you're caught in the middle?" she asked.

"I was never a part of all this until my accident forced me to be. Nowadays, I'm just trying to make sure that our bulls have a place to shine. Not only so they can be rodeo athletes in their own right, but also so we can attract other breeders who are looking to produce their own bloodlines from our championship bulls. I think that's where the future of this ranch is. Rick sees the bigger picture and has a good handle on making it all work."

"What is stopping your father from retiring?" Reba asked.

"I think he wants to see the ranch settled both in the rodeo as well as with selling cattle at auction. It's why it's going to be so hard to convince him to agree to the UPRC's exclusive terms. In the long run, I think it can only benefit us. In the short run, we might take a small monetary hit. But Rick and I have prepared for that. We've got enough of a nest egg that we could weather a few rough years."

"The contract is for five years," Reba said.

Shane winced. "Yeah, that's the problem. We're either going to suffer for a couple years, and then bounce back or we're going to tank completely. I'm hoping this may be the big break we're looking for. But it's a gamble, and my father is not a gambling man."

"What can I do to help?" she asked.

"Honestly just by you being in the room, it guarantees he's not going to fly off the handle. He'll be concentrating on making a good impression on you. Not because he thinks you and I are together, it's because he's hoping to pick your brains for some free veterinarian services."

"Are we together?" she teased.

"I think so."

Pleasure tickled up from her toes all the way to her ears and Reba wanted to wiggle with happiness. "I was hoping you'd said that."

"Good, because I don't want to be near you when you grab the castration tools."

Reba wished that they had a couple more days to spend on the farm. She would have liked to have gotten to know Lainey a little bit better. And she wouldn't even mind taking a look at some of the pregnant cows.

Shane

LATER ON THAT night, the whole family was sitting around the dinner table, eating the most delicious fried chicken and biscuits that Shane had ever experienced. Lainey had outdone herself.

"Lainey, this is amazing. You've got to give me the recipe for the spice blend. My dad will go crazy for this. He's a fried chicken connoisseur," Reba said.

Lainey flushed with delight. "I'd be glad to. So he's a big fan of fried chicken?"

"He dragged my mother to New Orleans one time, and all they did was eat fried chicken at every restaurant that served it. He had scoresheet that he kept in a notebook and took detailed notes on who had the best-tasting fried chicken New Orleans."

That didn't sound like a bad trip. Shane wondered when the rodeo season ended if Reba would be up for a trip like that.

"What was the verdict?" Bill asked.

"You'd have to ask him," Reba said. "All I know is my mother couldn't eat fried chicken for a whole year after that."

"I'll tell you what," Lainey said, "I'll give you my recipe for chicken fried steak, too. That way, she can change it up a bit."

"Speaking of steak," Bill said.

Shane caught Reba's gaze and rolled his eyes.

And because Bill couldn't help himself, they spent the next half an hour discussing care and prevention of his cattle from getting any of the common diseases.

"Dad." Rick groaned after about fifteen minutes more of cross-examination.

"All right, all right," Bill said. "Reba, you're a delight for indulging this old man. You're welcome back anytime. Don't bring kittens with you next time, though."

"Yeah," Lainey said. "Next time, we need bunnies and puppies."

"I'll keep my ear out," Reba said, delighted.

They thought she was joking. Shane had a feeling they were going to be in for a big surprise if someone dumped a litter of puppies near Reba.

But they had procrastinated this discussion long enough. Shane needed an answer to take to Jackson Blevins. He hoped it was going to be the correct one.

"So, Mom and Dad," Shane said. "You've had some time to review the contract. Rick and I have gone over any of the issues we think could come up with the exclusive contract. I think we should do it. So does Rick. Can we get you to sign off on it?"

"I don't have a problem with it," Mary said.

Shane smiled and did a small fist pump under the table.

Bill continued to eat his dinner and, for one annoying moment, Shane thought he was going to pretend that he hadn't heard Shane's question. But after he was done chewing his mouthful of chicken, he said, "I don't like it. The UPRC is too new of an organization to trust our bulls to exclusively. If they were willing to have us without being exclusive, of course, I'm all for that."

"They're getting away from non-exclusivity," Shane

said.

"That's because of that doping scandal last year, right?" Bill asked.

They had gone over this. Shane gave a curt nod.

"I don't see what the problem is. Our bulls are clean. They've always been clean. We've never had a problem with our bulls. If the testing is becoming too expensive, all they have to do is stop testing our bulls. Right, Reba?"

"Right," Reba said. "However, their insurance company is not going to let that happen. Maybe in the future, but not right now." She shrugged. "At least, that's the scuttlebutt I've been hearing. My sister, Dolly, says that the UPRC is very concerned about getting their attendance numbers up. So they want the best bulls that they can get. The more exciting the bulls, the more people are going to come out to watch them. It's a great honor for the Viking Ranch to be chosen, especially since you're relative newcomers in the field."

Shane groaned. *That was the wrong thing to say.*

"Newcomers? My daddy's been doing this, and his daddy was doing it for generations now."

"That's not what I meant," Reba said hurriedly. "I meant new to the UPRC."

"Our reputation is spotless. Always has been. Always will be. We're a family-owned ranch. We don't do any of these new-fangled treatments that could be construed as altering bulls' performance with drugs."

"Of course not," Reba said soothingly, but she had opened up a can of worms.

"I don't think it's a good idea." Bill shook his head.

Shane set his jaw and looked at Rick, hoping for back-up. Rick looked at his plate. *Dammit, Rick!* "If we don't sign with UPRC, we're not going to be able to command a higher price for our bulls at the other rodeos."

"So what?" Bill said. "We'll just apply to more rodeos, then."

That would make Shane's job a whole lot harder. "Even then, we're not guaranteed to get in those other rodeos. You want to negotiate from a position of strength. If we achieve the level of being an exclusive supplier to be UPRC, then in five years when our contract is up, that's going to make us more attractive to the other rodeos if we decide to diversify at that time."

"So you want me to hold my dick—sorry, ladies—sit on my hands for five years until this happens? I don't want to wait another five years to retire."

"Then don't," Shane said. "You've been training Rick and I to take over the business since we were kids. You know we're ready to take over. You just need to trust us enough to make the difficult decisions. Rick and I have talked about this, and we've considered all of the risks. Rick and I think we should do this. Don't we, Rick?" He gave his brother a significant look.

Now is the time to step the fuck up.

There was a tense moment when his father looked over at Rick, and Shane thought that Rick was going to capitulate and agree with his father. But Rick nodded and said, "Giving the UPRC exclusive rights for the next five years is the best decision we can make for the Viking Ranch's breeding program and for our stock trade."

Shane let out a slow breath and wanted to reach over and grip Reba's hand, but he didn't want to distract from what was going on at the table.

"Reba, do you think my sons are right and I should give the UPRC their exclusive?"

Reba looked uncomfortable and he was sorry that his father had put her in an awkward position, but she rallied and said, "Shane and Rick believe it is. And they have nothing but the best interests of the ranch in mind. They want it to succeed just as much as you do."

"It's their future," Bill said. "That's why it's so important."

Reba nodded.

Bill took a deep breath and crossed his arms over his chest. "All right, we'll do it your way. We'll see how it goes, and if I like what I see, maybe I'll retire down to Florida before next season."

"You don't have to go to Florida, if you don't want to," Shane said. "You can just retire on the ranch."

"What's the point of retiring, if you don't get to sit your butt on a boat and fish all day?"

"Amen," Mary said. "There's a marlin with my name on it."

Bill beamed at her.

Shane whooped and he and Rick high-fived across the table.

"All right, settle down," Mary said.

But then Rick went over and lifted their mom out of her chair and swung her around.

"Stop. I'm going to be dizzy," she said.

Dessert was a peach cobbler that Lainey had baked, and Shane thought again that Rick was a fool for not marrying her. But that was none of his business.

If the UPRC worked out for them they could all start looking to the future. Shane glanced over at Reba. And see about who they could spend it with. He and his ex-wife had already gotten hitched in Vegas before Shane had taken her home to meet his family. It hadn't started things off on the right foot. He and Reba were a long way away from marriage, but this could be the start of something great. Sure, he wasn't ever going to be a bull-riding rodeo star again, but a successful bull breeder wasn't bad boyfriend material.

Chapter Twelve

Shane

Fort Worth, TX

AFTER A BRUTAL red-eye flight, Shane and Reba went their separate ways once they reached the Fort Worth rodeo. He barely saw her for the rest of the morning, but they texted each other back and forth. They had tentative plans to go out for dinner tonight, although Shane didn't think he was going to make it much further beyond that before face-planting into a pillow.

He was going to order a bottle of wine, however, to celebrate officially being in the UPRC. His father had signed the contract last night, and Shane had forwarded it over to Jackson Blevins before he and Reba boarded the plane. He would wait until it was announced before he revoked his bids with the other rodeos for next season. They would definitely be running at a loss this year, but Shane was hoping that they would pick up some breeding clients to ease the pinch.

It was business as usual as Shane and Pat got the bulls ready for the testing. When the testing was over, they brought them to the bullpen for the rider's lottery. Shane was surprised when Ronnie Sunderland picked Sverre's name in the ballot, and instead of casting it back, Ronnie decided that he was going to ride him.

Shane applauded and went over to talk to him after all the other bull riders had picked their bulls and did any substitutions and trades before the final roster went to the announcers.

Shane walked over to him. "Look at the balls on you," he said, shaking his hand.

"Today's the day I'm going to ride your bull for eight seconds."

"I wish you all the luck in the world, Ronnie. Give him a hell of a ride."

If today was the day Sverre was going to lose his winning streak, it couldn't happen with a nicer cowboy than Ronnie Sunderland. Shane knew it was petty to think this, but Ronnie was worthy of the bull and a couple of the other guys weren't. He certainly wouldn't want Keith Kilgore to have the bragging rights for that. And Sverre would probably damn near kill Taylor or Nash. Vidar was deemed well enough to ride, Ingvar and Torkel had been chosen as well. Shane was looking forward to seeing how they would do statistic wise.

When he set up to watch the bull riders, he noticed that Taylor was bullfighting today with his father, Barney. Shane wondered if that meant that Taylor had made his decision about concentrating on being a bullfighter over being a bull rider.

The first bull rider up was Nash Weaver. He was riding Vidar. They had barely gotten out of the chute before the bull tossed him off. Maybe next time, Shane would record it on his phone so he could watch the ride in slow motion later. There was something about Nash's performance that bothered him. He was certainly not seating himself correctly on the bull. Maybe there were few tips he could give Nash. Or maybe Shane should mind his own fucking business. No one asked him his opinion.

"Hey, sugar," Abigail said, sitting down way too close to him. She was dressed in a leather bikini top with tight white shorts and cowboy boots. She had on enough turquoise and silver jewelry to set off metal detectors at fifty feet.

"I just love watching bull riders," she said. "You know that makes me horny as hell."

"I'm sure Keith is thrilled by that," Shane said, removing her hand from where she'd placed it on his knee.

"Keith is going to be busy for the next hour and a half. Why you and I go see what trouble we can get into my camper?" Abigail said, running a sharp red nail down his arm.

"You know that Keith is looking right at us," Shane said.

Abigail whipped her head to where the bull riders were waiting their turn to ride, and sure enough, her fiancé was scowling up at them. She simpered and waved at him, but it didn't change the sour expression on his face.

"Why are you like this?" Shane asked. He honestly wanted to know. "Keith seems to be everything that you want. Why do you want to risk fucking it up by sleeping with me?"

"Don't act like Keith is the wronged party here," she said grumpily. "I know what goes on in the bars when I'm not on the circuit with him."

"So you're saying you and Keith have an open relationship?" *Why was he even having this conversation?*

"No, of course not."

"If you both want to screw around, why not?"

"Then he's not going to want to marry me."

"I've got news for you, sweetheart, if he's fucking around on you, he doesn't want to marry you anyway."

"You're an asshole—you know that?" Abigail got up angrily and stormed away.

"Yeah." He sighed. "I've heard that before." And from her.

His other bulls did really good. Ingvar tossed his rider. Torkel was ridden for eight seconds, but he kicked and whirled like a champion. Both he and his rider, Jennings, got a great score. Shane was proud of them.

And then it was time for Sverre and Ronnie. Shane got his phone ready. His father always loved to see Sverre in action. Out of the gate, Ronnie looked strong. He was seated well and had a good grip on the rope. His form was impeccable. He could do it.

Sverre was a maniac. He kicked and whirled. Bucking hard, Sverre tossed Ronnie who flipped over the bull's head. Sverre nailed him with his horns on the way down. Shane winced at the hard shot Ronnie took in the back. Landing on his hands and knees, Ronnie was in a bad position. Sverre jumped and landed on him. What the hell? Sverre was unreasonably pissed off. Ronnie crumpled, his neck at a terrible angle. Shane shot to his feet, his phone falling to the ground.

Taylor and Barney rushed in. Sverre stomped on Ronnie again and kicked out at Taylor, nailing him in the chest. Taylor was flung back and landed on his ass. Scrambling up, he went back in. His chest protector mitigated most of the blow, but he would still be black and blue later. Sverre shook his head and lunged at Barney with his horns. Barney held on while Taylor covered Ronnie's body to protect him as the paramedics waited for it to be clear to come in. Ronnie wasn't moving.

"Shit," Shane muttered. He hoped Ronnie was all right.

The pickup rider got a rope around Sverre and between him, Barney, and another bullfighter, they muscled the ornery son of a bitch back through the chute. The paramedics rushed in. Shane had a bad feeling in his stomach.

By the time Shane pushed his way through the hysterical crowd to the backstage area, they had loaded Ronnie and his wife Vanessa into the back of the ambulance. As the ambulance sped away, Shane caught Barney's eye. Barney shook his head in a slow, mournful no. Shane's stomach dropped. *Fuck.*

"That bull of yours is a menace," Keith Kilgore said grabbing Shane by the shirt.

Shane knocked his hand away and shoved him back. "Back off," he said.

Keith went at him again, but Nash was suddenly there. He held Keith in a half nelson and pretty much perpwalked him out of the area.

"You should see to your bull," Barney said under his

breath and patted him on the shoulder.

The raucous cheers and pulsating music that filled the air felt distant and muffled to Shane. It wasn't strange that the rodeo went on with their events like nothing had happened. And yet, as he wandered around the barn and animal pens waiting for news about Ronnie, it all felt disrespectful.

When Barney found him a few minutes later, Shane was sitting on the ground by the pen that Sverre was in. Barney's face was solemn and Shane's heart sank, a wave of foreboding washing over him. He had harbored a hope that Ronnie would be okay, but the look on Barney's face confirmed what they both had known when the ambulance had pulled away.

"He's gone," Barney said the words. "Dead on arrival."

A heaviness settled in Shane's chest, and he fought to steady himself. "Damn it. This wasn't supposed to happen." Shane put his head in his hands. No one ever wanted to hear news like that.

"As you can imagine, the boys are devastated. They might come here looking for revenge." Barney eyed Sverre warily.

While they all knew the risks of riding a bull, it was rare that it would end in death. Broken collarbone, a broken leg, sure. One of their own dying was a solemn occasion that put the fear of mortality in a lot of bull riders. And anger could simmer into something more dangerous.

"Ronnie wouldn't want that," Taylor said, coming up alongside of his father. "Sverre isn't a murderer. He's just a bull."

He looked up at the sound of running feet. Ready to defend his bull if he had to, Shane clenched his fists. But he was relieved to see Reba as she flung herself into his arms.

"I just heard," she said, out of breath. "I ran all the way here."

"Were all the golf carts taken?" he said, trying for a joke.

"We'll go back and try and keep the peace," Barney said.

"It's not your fault," Taylor said.

Shane nodded at them over Reba's head, grateful that they came to see him, even as they were dealing with their own grief. Ronnie had been a good man. He had been well liked. Shane—and everyone else—was going to miss him.

"I'm so, so sorry about Ronnie," Reba said. "How are you doing?"

"Shitty," he said. "But it's better now that you're here." His phone buzzed. He didn't want talk to anyone right now, but this was Jackson Blevins.

"Yeah," Shane said.

"Shane, we got a problem."

"I'll make sure that Sverre is no longer at the events for the rest of the season."

"Don't be hasty," Blevins said. "He's still a fine bull. I will be pleased to have him at the next rodeo. But Vanessa Sunderland is saying that the bull was doped up."

"That's ridiculous," Shane said.

"That's what I was hoping to hear," Blevins said. "We're going to run the tests again."

"That's fine. You're not going to find anything. My

bulls are clean."

Reba's head jerked up. "Of course, they are. I ran your tests myself this morning. They were perfectly fine."

"Who's that?" Blevins said.

"That's Reba Keller. She's one of the UPRC veterinarians."

"I know the Keller family very well. Her words will go a long way to settling down the rumors. I'll talk to her sister, Dolly, and let her know that Reba tested your bull herself."

"Thank you," Shane said, but Blevins had already hung up.

"I should've taken a golf cart," Reba said. "I'd have all my stuff right now. Give me about half an hour and I'll be back with everything, and then I'll run the tests on Sverre again."

"I know he was clean when I brought him up here this morning. Could he have been injected with something in between the time your test happened and the time Ronnie got on him?"

"I don't know," Reba said. "We'll have to check with security and see if there's been anybody back with the bulls who shouldn't have been."

"I'll do that," Shane said.

While Reba went to get her equipment, Shane called Pat who had been resting in his truck and had missed everything. Shane filled him in on what had happened.

"Oh shit, I'll be right there," Pat said.

"Were you back in the bull area?"

"No, boss, I wasn't. I think from now on one of us should be."

Shane was kicking himself. After the accident with Vidar, he should have insisted on it. He should have been there. He hoped that nothing had been introduced into Sverre's system. For Ronnie's sake, but also for the bull's. He hated the poison that some people jacked up their animals with. Sverre didn't need any chemicals to be a good athlete, and it sickened him that someone thought they could get away with hurting anyone on the circuit, whether it was an animal or rider. He couldn't figure out any motivation to inject Sverre with a performance-enhancing drug.

Pat and Reba arrived about the same time. Reba took Sverre's sample and then said, "If it's okay, I'd like to retest all of your stock?"

Shane nodded. "Do what you have to do."

"I'm going to have to cancel dinner tonight," she said. "I want to oversee these lab results personally."

"Call me as soon as you get an answer," he said.

Shane and Pat stood guard until the rodeo was over. They loaded up their bulls into the trailer.

"Pat, I want you to get on the road right away. I'll call ahead to our friends at the Brady Cattle Ranch so they know to expect you a little earlier than planned. I'm afraid things are going to get ugly if we stay overnight and then leave in the morning like we had planned."

"You got it."

"I may need you to fly back to Montana tomorrow morning if we need to find a bull to replace Sverre. You'd have to drive back down to Brady with him. If that turns out to be the case, just bring Rick with you so he can take

Sverre back. I'll fill him in with the details so you don't have to."

"This is a hell of a thing," Pat said.

"Yes, it is. Drive safe. Call me when you get there."

He watched the bulls while Pat grabbed some dinner and coffee to go. He called his brother and filled him in. Rick would break the news to his parents. They hadn't been watching the rodeo, thankfully.

The press hadn't been allowed back in the bullpens, but it was only a matter of time before one of them snuck in. Shane didn't relax until Pat had left the arena and called to tell him he was on the highway.

After that, Shane didn't know what to do with himself. He didn't want to pester Reba and he knew he wouldn't be welcome company to any bull riders tonight. He was surprised, however, to find Abigail in the horse barn when he wandered in. She was taking care of Ronnie's horse, Starshine. She'd always loved horses. He could see she'd been crying. She looked up when he approached.

"Well, your bull is still undefeated."

"Knock that shit off," he said, gently.

She burst into tears and threw herself into Shane's arms. "It could have been Keith. He wanted that damned bull so bad. He was pissed that Ronnie pulled Sverre and wouldn't trade."

Shane patted her back awkwardly, as if a few hours ago she hadn't been propositioning him so she could cheat on Keith. He would never understand Abigail, but he did understand that she was scared. She had cried when Shane had his wreck and rode to the hospital in an ambulance with him.

"I just can't believe it. Poor Vanessa. What is she going to do now?"

"It won't be easy," he said. "But she's a strong woman. She'll survive this."

"I need a drink," she said, rubbing his back. "Keith and the boys don't want to be disturbed. How about you and I get lost in the bottom of a bottle?"

It was tempting. But he knew that drinking got Abigail horny almost as much as watching bull riders did.

"I don't think that's a good idea."

She clung to him tighter. "I think it's a great idea."

Reba

REBA WAS SURPRISED when Diane burst into the veterinarian trailer while she was waiting for the results to finish.

"I need to talk to Reba alone. Take the ten minutes," Diane said to Dr. Victor and the two vet techs who were still there, packing up the gear for travel.

"What's up?" Reba asked when they had cleared out. She was dead on her feet, but she wasn't going to rest until the lab results were done.

"Are you standing behind your findings that Shane Calland's bull Sverre was not given any performance-enhancing drugs?"

"That's right. I'm running a second test to verify now. What's this all about?"

"Are you sleeping with him?"

"That's none of your damn business." Reba put her hands on her hips.

"It is, if he's being accused of drugging his bulls and you are the veterinarian in charge of the test results."

Reba felt like someone had slapped her across the face. "How dare you accuse me of falsifying records. I've never done anything like that in my life." Damn it, it was just like being back in Dr. Kilgore's review meeting. She was automatically in the wrong. Reba hated that feeling—then and now.

"I'm not accusing you of anything," Diane said. "But you have to admit, it looks suspicious."

"Bullshit," Reba said. "My relationship with Shane has nothing to do with the test results. I wouldn't lie for him. I wouldn't lie for anyone who was hurting animals. And you should know that. Shane is a good man. He did not dope up his bulls. He doesn't need to. Maybe instead of this being a witch hunt and everybody pointing fingers at Shane, we should start to look and see who would gain the most if Shane's bulls failed."

"Now you're sounding like you have some conspiracy theories."

"Can you blame me? I'm feeling a little bit paranoid here because you're accusing me of shit that I didn't do."

"Reba, no one is accusing you of anything. But before they do, I don't want you to test any more bulls. And these results won't mean anything."

"I didn't do anything wrong," Reba said. Not back then and certainly not right now. But it didn't matter, did it?

"And now, no one can accuse you of favoritism, or worse falsifying records, since you're no longer going to be involved with testing bulls."

"So what am I supposed to do? Sit on my thumbs while the rest the team does double work?"

"There are plenty of things for you to do at the rodeos. There's always going to be horses needing assistance, as well as the minor things that come up throughout the week. But you're off of bull duty."

"That's not fair, and you know it. It shouldn't matter who I'm sleeping or not sleeping with."

"I agree," Diane said. "But it does matter. You don't want to have the gossips ruin your reputation. So humor me and keep your career on track. I'm doing this to protect you."

"Really?" Reba said. "Because it sounds like you're covering your ass."

"That, too," Diane said. "The two aren't mutually exclusive."

"This is a demotion. It's bullshit and unfair." And it felt exactly like it had when no one believed her that Dr. Kilgore behaved inappropriately.

"I'm sorry you feel that way."

"How am I supposed to feel? If I hadn't been dating Shane, would this conversation have ever happened?"

"No."

"Then I'm guilty until proven innocent. Who told you about us?" Reba asked. "We haven't been together long."

"That doesn't matter."

"It does if someone is trying to set me or Shane up."

"Are you listening to yourself? You sound ultra-paranoid. Reba, it's just for a little while. If it doesn't happen again, we can revisit your job duties in a few months. And if it does happen again, you have a chance of saving your reputation by not being directly involved with the testing."

"Shane didn't drug his bulls."

"I hope you're right." Diane said. "I'll have someone look at these final results and let you know the outcome. Report to my office when you get to Odessa."

It took everything in her not to slam the trailer door when Reba stormed out. Dr. Victor was hanging out nearby and he looked like he was going to say something to her, but she glared at him until he thought better of it.

This was utter bullshit. It must have something to do with UPRC limiting the breeders down to only three. This had to be the work of a rival breeder trying to discredit Shane. And the worst part of all of this was Ronnie Sunderland died because of somebody's greed. Reba knew in her heart that Shane hadn't drugged the bull.

Reba called Dolly to let her know what was going on. She was glad when Dolly shouted, "That's a load of horseshit." It felt good that her sister had her back.

"What are you going to do?" Dolly said, immediately meeting her at the beer tent.

"I've half a mind to just up and quit," Reba said. "But aside from this recent nonsense, I really did like this job."

"Do you want me to ask around to other rodeos?" Dolly asked.

"I can do that myself," Reba said. "I'm pissed off, but I'm not at that level of pissed off just yet. If worst comes to worst, I can always ask Lou if he wants to hire me on. Maybe even Shane's family would be interested in having me on staff."

Her heart fluttered a little at the thought of going back to Montana.

"Honey, I don't think either one of them can afford a full-time vet. You'd be back to traveling around the states going to various rodeos, filling in when needed."

Just what she didn't want to do. Go backwards. She was not going back to an office. That was for damned sure.

"Keep your head down. Do the job they want you to do. They're not going to cut your salary, are they?"

"Diane didn't mention it."

"Then suck it up for a few weeks and do the grunt work. They'll put you back in the lab when the other doc gets sick of covering for you."

"I guess you're right," Reba grumbled. It still pissed her off, though. This had been her dream job and one little stumble had turned it into a nightmare. She had to wonder, though, if there was something bigger going on that she wasn't aware of. She walked back to the veterinary trailer to grab her purse that she had left inside before going home to her kitten-less RV. She missed the little fuzz balls already.

She opened the trailer door and Dr. Victor turned in surprise. "What are you doing back here?"

"Just getting my purse. I'm on call tonight anyway while everyone's packing up to leave. Did you get roped into checking the results?"

"Yeah, they're still working." The in-house testing that they did took a few hours.

"Can you let me know when they're done?"

Victor shook his head. "Diane asked me not to share them with anyone, but I'm sure you can call her tomorrow morning."

"Yeah," Reba said, stuffing down the frustration. "Have a nice night." She didn't want to take out her bad mood on him. It wasn't his fault she had been taken off the testing.

She was surprised to see Dolly still waiting outside for her.

"I've got to go and get some action shots of Sverre," she said. "Jackson Blevins wants to put some videos out on YouTube. I guess he's trying to mitigate the bad press. At least, I hope so," Dolly muttered.

"Let's take the golf cart," Reba said, snatching the keys. Since she was on call, she wanted to have her kit with her in case something exciting happened. Although, they all could probably do with a little less excitement around here.

"It's a shit show tonight," Dolly said sadly.

In the after hours of the rodeo, there was usually a party atmosphere. But tonight, there was a solemn pall over everything.

"A few of the cowboys started a small bonfire and a bunch of people are toasting Ronnie Sunderland and sharing stories."

"That's nice," Reba said.

"And then there's the dumbasses who are picking fights with each other and grieving that way."

"It's understandable," Reba said.

"It's dangerous, that's what it is." Dolly wrapped her sweater around herself and shuddered. "Poor Vanessa. Poor Ronnie."

"Poor Shane."

"Him, too." Dolly sighed. "This really sucks. Especially, when I think about LeAnn riding a bull."

"Don't even go there," Reba said.

"I know. I can't help it."

As they drove by the horse barn, they saw Shane storming out of it with a buckle bunny chasing after him.

"Don't you walk away from me, Shane Calland."

"Oh shit," Dolly said. "That's his ex-wife, Abigail. She's engaged to Keith Kilgore."

Reba made a face. She hoped Keith wasn't around. That would be the cherry on the shit sundae if she ran into him or his uncle. Hopefully, Dr. Kilgore was back in Paris, Texas.

"Abigail, go home," Shane said, turning toward her.

That was when Abigail flung herself into Shane's arms and kissed him.

"Don't run her over," Dolly said, hanging on for dear life as Reba put her foot down on the pedal. But by the time it took for the little golf cart to burst forward, Shane had put Abigail out at arm's length.

"No, Abigail. It ain't happening. I'm not interested. I know you're hurting and you're sad. I am, too. But you are not the one I want to be with."

"Oh shit, this is some next-level drama," Dolly said.

Reba pulled up alongside the couple. "Going my way,

cowboy?" she asked.

"Definitely." Shane climbed into the back seat of the golf cart.

His ass had barely touched down when Reba put her foot back on the gas pedal. She resisted the urge to flip off his ex-wife.

"Thanks for the rescue," he said. "I'd like to say she's not normally like that and this is all just the reaction to Ronnie's death, but she's always like that. I'm sorry you had to see that."

"I'm not," Reba said.

It proved to her that Shane wasn't the same party animal that he had been when he was on the circuit. He could have taken what Abigail was offering, and yet he didn't. They hadn't even had the "exclusive" talk yet, so she couldn't have blamed him. And yet, it warmed her heart that he hadn't wanted to kiss his ex.

"I'm Dolly," her sister said, holding out her hand to shake. "I'm sorry about what happened today."

"Thank you. It's rough for everyone."

"I'm going to need to be an intrusive bitch. Jackson Blevins wants some footage of Sverre. I know you probably mind like hell. If I could get out of it, I would. But it could help ease some tensions from outside publicity if I could take some pictures of Sverre tonight."

"Sorry," Shane said. "He's already gone and on his way to Brady."

"What's in Brady?" Reba asked.

"We rent a pasture on a farm out there when we're at the Texas rodeos. It's about four hours, give or take, from anywhere we need to be. It beats driving twenty-four hours straight back home. Although"—he rubbed the back of his neck wearily—"I considered it after today."

"Have you talked to your family?" Reba asked.

"Yeah, they're devastated. They want to bring Sverre home. I'm not sure what the UPRC wants to do yet. Jackson Blevins wants to have a conference call with me tomorrow. I'm not sure what he's going to say. He's the boss. We'll do what he wants."

"He is at that," Dolly said. "Anyway, we'll find a way to make things right for Ronnie and Vanessa."

"And Sverre," Reba said.

"Him, too."

"Do you think you could give me the address to your Brady farm and permission to let me and a camera crew visit to film Sverre tomorrow?" Dolly asked.

"I'll call the farm. I'm not sure about the timing, though. He might be going back to Montana in the next few days."

"Whatever you can arrange would be great. Reba, can I bunk with you tonight?"

Reba really wanted some alone time with Shane and opened her mouth to say that to her sister, but Shane squeezed her hand.

"I'm not going to be great company tonight. I think I'm going to curl up with a bottle of whiskey and drink myself to sleep. I'm exhausted, so it shouldn't take too long."

"Oh, okay." A little pang of hurt lodged in her chest. She had wanted to be there for him, and if she was honest she wanted to sleep in his arms tonight and be comforted because of the feelings Diane's bullshit had brought up. But she shouldn't be so selfish.

"Just drop me off at the front office," Dolly said. "I've got to grab a few things. I'll meet you back at the Winnebago."

She swung the golf cart around and drove to the main area. After Dolly hopped off, Shane came around and sat next to her.

"This has been a real shitty day." He slung his arm around her. "Thanks for being here for me. Do you want to grab a beer while we wait for the test results?"

"About that," Reba sighed. "My boss kicked me off the drug testing because I'm sleeping with you."

"Shit." Shane hugged her to him. "I'm so fucking sorry."

It felt great to be hugged. "It's not your fault. I'd like to know how they found out we were together."

"Fucking cowboys gossip like it's their job," he grumbled.

"You'll probably find out the test results before I do," she said. "But if I hear anything I'll let you know. I wish I wasn't on call tonight. I'd join you in that bottle of whiskey."

"It's not going to be a pretty sight."

"I'm not just in this for the parties and the great sex." She tipped her head back and kissed him. The tingles she felt when their lips touched washed away some of the blues. She realized she was tired as hell, too. "I'm here for you."

"I appreciate that," he said, touching his forehead

against hers. "I'm not used to someone like you. Abigail bolted at the first sign of trouble."

"I'm not Abigail."

"And thank God for that," he said. "I'll make it up to you in Odessa, I promise."

"I'll make sure Dolly gets a hotel room."

They shared a grin.

"I'm sorry again about your job."

"It'll blow over. Things will get back to normal."

"Not for Vanessa," Shane said sadly.

Reba hadn't liked her, but she wouldn't have wished this on anyone. "No, I guess not. Ronnie was a great guy."

Reba drove him back to where his truck was parked. "Don't drink and drive. Call me if you need me."

"I do need you." He gave her another toe-curling kiss and then reluctantly got into his truck. As she watched him drive away, hurting for him and for Vanessa, Reba realized that she needed him, too.

Chapter Thirteen

JACKSON BLEVINS WAS being inundated with meetings, but at least they were video calls, so he didn't have to stop his extracurricular activities. He just made sure Debbi had on her sound-canceling headset on while she blew him. As long as the camera on his computer showed him from the neck up and Debbi didn't use her teeth, everything would be all good.

He poured himself a glass of whiskey and rested his hand on Debbi's head, making sure she took him all the way down her throat. First up was Dolly Keller. Too damned bad, it wasn't her on her knees in front of him. It would have been a dream come true, especially if she wore her cheerleader outfit. *Rah, rah sis-boom-bah, indeed.*

"Everyone has been real supportive of Vanessa," Dolly said, wiping the tears from the corners of her eyes.

"Yeah, yeah, what's the buzz about Sverre?"

She took a shuddering breath. "Well, there's calls for him to be put down and PETA is up in arms about it."

"Good, good."

"What?" she said, her voice sharpening.

"All publicity is good publicity," he said.

"Not really."

Jackson didn't like being contradicted, but Debbi's mouth was taking the edge off things. He sipped his whiskey, still wishing Dolly was there in person. She had a rack like her namesake, and he would have loved a closer look. Unfortunately, her camera was viewing from the neck up as well.

"Sverre's tests have come back and he's clean. Your sister can confirm that," he said.

Dolly snorted. "No, she can't. She's been taken off the testing."

"What?" Jackson barked, shifting in his chair as Debbi increased pace. He yanked back on her hair. "Why?"

"It's because she has a relationship with Shane Calland," Dolly said reluctantly.

No shit. That was why he wanted her reviewing the test results. She wouldn't want to get her new boyfriend in trouble. "Who's fucking decision was that?"

"I don't know. I guess her boss."

Maybe having Reba Keller away from the testing was good for this week. An idea came to him suddenly. It was brilliant. He was brilliant.

"Well, that's bullshit. You tell your sister that she'll be back doing the testing soon. I'll make sure of it."

Dolly blinked. "Thank you. I really appreciate that, sir."

He liked being called sir and he forced Debbi's head down until she gagged. Yeah, that was it. He took a shuddering breath. "No problem. You can do something for me now."

"Anything."

Oh yeah, he really liked the sound of that.

"I need you to arrange a special event for Odessa."

Dolly nodded. "You got it. What did you have in mind?"

"We're going to put your sister LeAnn on Sverre."

"What?" Dolly snapped.

"I want you to bill it as Killer on a killer." Jackson moved his hand across the camera as if he was reading it on a marquee.

"That's really in poor taste," she said.

"I didn't ask your opinion," he said sourly. Dolly was killing his buzz. He drank a few swallows of whiskey to get his groove back. "Get it done. I want people talking about this. Good or bad. I don't care."

"I'm not sure that's a good idea."

"Hey, when I want to know your opinion, I'll give it to you. Get it done." He hung up on her. Yeah, Reba Keller might have second thoughts about putting her baby sister on a bull that was full of rage-producing steroids. This would work out better if she was out of the testing altogether for Odessa. Once Sverre took out LeAnn, Jackson would demand the bull be put down. Then, he'd put Reba back in charge of covering for her fuck buddy.

He let Debbie suck him off until he came down her throat while he thought about all the money he was about to make.

"Thanks, babe," he said when he was done. Luckily the Viagra had kicked in because he had another call. He lifted her headphones briefly off her ears. "Take off your clothes and bend over the desk. I'll be with you in a minute." He replaced them and gave her tits a little squeeze. She giggled at him.

While she stripped, he dialed his man on the inside. This time, he kept the camera off.

"Great job with Sverre. I need you to do it again for Odessa. We've got a big exhibition event planned for him and I want him insane when the rider gets on him. Just like we did on Mick's bull last year. Don't worry, I've got you covered on the tests. You can drug him anytime. You don't have to wait."

Debbie's ass looked nice and juicy as she positioned herself in front of him. He hit mute when he poked a finger in her to make sure she was lubed up.

"Oh." She moaned.

"Quiet," he said, smacking her ass.

"You got it, boss," his man on the inside said. "I thought we were going to have trouble with Reba Keller, but when I told Diane that she was fucking Calland, she took her off the project."

Jackson toggled off mute. "No one asked you to do that." Just because it worked out this time, didn't mean the next time he improvised on his orders wouldn't be a disaster. "Do what you're told. No more. No less."

"Sorry."

"And don't get caught."

He hung up the phone and then he raw-dogged Debbi. He waited until he was finished before making his last phone call. "Take a hike," he said, when she took off the headphones. He sank back into his chair. "Get me some lunch."

"Yes, sir," Debbi said, stepping back into her panties.

"I said get out of here." He tossed her bra at her. "I've got to make an important call."

She hurried out of his office, holding her heels and her clothes. She was a stupid heifer, but she could suck the chrome off a trailer hitch.

He called his bookie once she shut the door behind her. "Ten thousand dollars on LeAnn Keller to get tossed off her bull on Saturday."

"She's been doing really well in the arenas. How sure of a bet is this? You know we've got several interested parties in this action," his bookie said.

"As long as they're willing to kick a little back to me for making this happen, I'll be glad to keep doing this. We made a mint on that Mickelson wreck last season, didn't we?" Jackson was still miffed that they missed having Killer Keller on the bull that time. It would have taken care of two problems. Getting Shelby Miller to back off on her women "athletes" permanently, as well as giving them a shitload of publicity.

He hoped, this time around, it paid off. He was sick of having women take the spotlights away from the real stars of the rodeo, the cowboys. And if Killer Keller met the same fate as Ronnie, well that was pure entertainment gold. Jackson opened up his special box and did a line of coke.

Things were looking up.

Chapter Fourteen

Reba

Fort Worth, TX
Monday before the Odessa Weekend Rodeo

REBA WASN'T IN the mood for the family meeting that Dolly had called tonight. She was left to pack up the veterinary trailer for the five-hour drive to Odessa. As it was, she was pulling double duty, still sitting in for Dr. Victor's on-call hours because she owed him one for when she went to Montana.

But Dolly had sounded almost hysterical on the phone and Reba owed her, too, for all the times she smoothed things over with free tickets or VIP passes. When she finally got to the Fort Worth Steak Emporium, she was the last to arrive. She was surprised to see that not only were LeAnn and Dylan there, but Shane was seated as well. That was a nice surprise, even if he looked as confused as she was that he was there.

"Hey, cowboy," she said, giving him a quick kiss on the lips.

LeAnn snickered and elbowed Dylan. "Kissy face."

"I thought you were heading out to Brady today," Reba

said, ignoring her sister.

"I got pulled into a bunch of meetings about Sverre and I didn't want to do it while driving."

"Sounds like the opposite of fun." She sat down next to him. "Sorry I'm late. Why are we all here?"

Dolly tapped a few buttons on her phone and all of their phones buzzed. "You need to see this before I send it out to the world. And before you start, this comes straight from Jackson Blevins himself."

"Killer on a killer?" LeAnn made a face. "That's awful. Vanessa doesn't need to deal with this shit now."

Reba couldn't believe that they were going to put LeAnn on Sverre. She couldn't even look at Shane. "You can't ride that bull."

"Okay, first of all, you're not my mama or my husband. You can't tell me what to do," LeAnn said.

"I can get your mama on the line," Reba said, waggling her phone at her sister. She didn't want to pull that card if she didn't have to, but for Pete's sake, a man just died from riding that bull.

"You can't ride Sverre," Dylan said.

"Fuck you. I can do what I want," LeAnn told him, and he was her husband.

"Let's not go there right now," Dolly said. She pinned Shane with a glare. "What's up with your bull? I watched his last ten rides over and over again today. He's tough and a ball buster, but he has never acted like that."

"I know," Shane said.

"His test results were clear," Dolly said.

Reba tried not to let her relief show on her face. She

knew that Shane would never drug his bulls. But she hadn't been sure someone else wouldn't have sabotaged Sverre because they were jealous of the contract.

"I know that, too. We don't do any of that shit with our bulls."

"Doesn't mean someone else wouldn't," Dylan said. "Dolly's right. Something got into your bull. He shouldn't be in the lottery until we can figure out what."

"I can give him a full exam," Reba said. "It's not like I'm doing anything else right now. I'm free until I have to report in at Odessa on Thursday."

Shane nodded. "I'd appreciate that. I told Blevins that I'd send Sverre home and give him another bull, but he didn't want that. I didn't expect him to do something as distasteful as this, though. Are you sure you have to go through with this?" he asked Dolly.

"I've got a call in to Shelby Miller. She's the only one who could override him and stop this. And even she might only be able to delay it for a while. I'm going to break the news to Vanessa after dinner. It's the least I could do."

"I'd like the chance to ride Sverre," LeAnn said.

"He's too much bull for you," Shane said. "And I'm not saying that because you're a woman. I'm saying that because he's kicked off more experienced bull riders."

"Not to mention he killed someone two days ago," Dolly said, and Reba heard the hysteria in her voice.

"If it comes to it, I'll wear the best protective equipment we can get," LeAnn said.

"I'll make sure the bullfighters are ready and prepared," Dylan said.

"I can't believe you're on board for this," Dolly said, scowling at him.

"Oh, I hate it," Dylan replied. "It's the stuff of nightmares. Ronnie's death has brought everything back for me when we lost Johnny Montana. I thought I was over the guilt."

"I'm sorry," LeAnn said, linking her fingers through his. "I didn't think. I'm being selfish. Maybe I won't ride this bull."

Dylan nodded tightly and looked down at the table.

"Finally, some sense." Reba slumped in her seat.

"But my contract with the UPRC says I have to do exhibitions like this when asked," LeAnn said.

"Let me work on that," Dolly said.

"If it needs to be another one of my bulls, Vidar and Torkel are good choices," Shane said.

Dolly made a few notes in her phone. "I'll see what I can do."

Dinner wasn't the relaxing or festive affair that it could have been, but Shane ordered a few expensive bottles of wine, and it took the edge off of things.

"I had wanted to celebrate tonight because the Viking Ranch has been chosen as one of the exclusive suppliers of bulls for the UPRC, but Blevins asked me to keep it on the down-low. I had thought it was because of the tragedy with Ronnie. But he doesn't give a shit about that if he's going to promo Killer on a killer."

"Why the secrecy?" Reba asked.

"Maybe they're waiting until the end of the season," LeAnn said.

"It's going to piss off a lot of people," Shane said.

Like Shane was fond of saying, cowboys like to gossip so it was probable that a few people already knew about it. Maybe they were even unhappy enough to try and hurt the Viking Ranch because of it.

Reba clinked glasses with him. "Good luck with the contract."

"We'll need it," he said.

After dinner, Dylan and LeAnn said they were going back home for a few days, but they would see them all in Odessa.

"I'll travel with Reba in the Winnebago to Brady tomorrow to take some pictures of Sverre."

Reba tried not to grimace. She had been hoping for a night with Shane since he was still in town, but that didn't look like it was in the cards for tonight either.

"I just need to grab some stuff," Reba said. It was a good thing the veterinarian trailer wasn't going to be picked up until the next morning. And that she was in charge of packing it up. She'd be able to grab the supplies she needed to run all the tests she wanted and to give Sverre a full exam.

"I'll go with you," Shane said.

At least they could spend a little time together alone tonight.

"Do you think it could be a virus or an allergic reaction?" Shane asked as he drove her back to the veterinarian's trailer.

"I don't know." Reba leaned her head on his arm. "If LeAnn does have to ride him, will you be there in the stall with her? I know Dylan will be, but it will ease my mind if you can be there, too."

"I will. I won't leave Sverre's side until the chute gate opens with her on it. Hopefully, it won't come to that."

"Thank you," she said.

"I'm sorry this whole situation has come back to bite you on the ass," Shane said. "I never thought you'd lose your job over being with me, and now your sister has to put her life on the line."

"You heard her back there. She wants the chance to go on Sverre. Like I said before, none of this your fault. And I didn't lose my job. Not yet anyway." They wouldn't look too kindly on what she was going to do with their supplies, though. With any luck, no one would ever find out. But she didn't care. It made her feel better to be proactive in this. "I still can't shake the feeling that this is somehow related to Vidar being hurt. I keep going over in my mind all the little things that don't add up. I'd like to pin it on Dr. Kilgore trying to muscle in on your exclusive contract, but I'm not sure how much of that is me wanting him to be the villain."

"His nephew is a prick, and I'm not just saying that because he's banging my ex-wife."

"She seemed awfully cozy with you before. Could Keith be taking out his jealousy on your bull?"

Shane parked by the trailer. "He's mean enough, but I think he's a chickenshit. He's afraid of the bulls. He doesn't go near them unless he can help it."

Reba thought about that as she waited to let Shane open the truck door for her. Now, she was kicking herself that she didn't find out what the job offer Keith had for her was. She had assumed it was on behalf of his uncle not having the guts to ask her to come back to work for him. Maybe she'd call Dr. Kilgore tomorrow and see what it was all about. She might be able to find some clues if he was a part of all of this. She slid out of the truck, grabbed her keys, and unlocked the trailer.

Shane slumped into a chair while Reba gathered what she needed. She grabbed a microscope, centrifuge, blood chemistry analyzer, urinalysis equipment, and other tools she would need for onsite testing. "I did catch Taylor Keating in the bullpens where he didn't belong. He said he was trying to get familiar with the bulls. I don't see him as the type to hurt them, though."

Reba took a deep breath as she remembered there was someone else to consider. "I caught Nash Weaver back there, too. He didn't have too good of a reason to be back there. And while he seems like a nice guy, there's something off about him. Dolly is suspicious of him because he has a hidden past."

Shane nodded. "He did come out of nowhere. It could be he's the one hurting the bulls, but for what purpose?"

"Maybe he's working for a rival bull breeder?" Reba double-checked her gear to make sure that she could do everything on the road. She'd put it all back before it was missed in Odessa. Shane helped her carry the duffel bags out of the trailer.

"I should have a talk with him in Odessa," Shane said grimly.

Reba got that same shiver of fear from the menace in

his voice. "We don't have any proof he's behind this."

"He's as good of a lead as any."

"Don't do anything rash."

"I will be the soul of discretion," Shane said, helping her stow her gear. He drove her back to her Winnebago where she made him a thermos of coffee.

"Help yourself to any road trip snacks," she said.

"I'm still full from dinner." He stepped in closer. "But I was hoping for a few kisses."

"Me, too." Reba sighed. She wrapped her arms around his neck and gave herself up to the sweet way his mouth moved on hers.

"When's Dolly coming back?" he muttered as she dragged him toward the bedroom.

"Who cares?" Reba said, unbuttoning his shirt.

"I don't mind, if you don't mind."

Right now, all she wanted was to feel his body sliding all over hers. She would have liked to have fallen asleep in his arms afterward, but she knew they didn't have that kind of time. This was going to have to be down and dirty and quick as hell, unfortunately. Stepping out of her jeans, she made quick work of undressing as they went into the bedroom. Shane tossed off his clothes and turned back to her.

Fortunately, he was as ready for her as she was for him. They didn't even make it to the bed. He put on a condom and then pressed her against the closed door. Reba wrapped her legs around his waist and he slid deep inside of her.

"Hello, beautiful." He sighed.

His hard length was satisfying and exactly what she had

been missing since they came back from Montana.

"Yes." She moaned, her toes curling as he slowly eased in and out of her.

The tips of her nipples brushed against the wiry hairs of his chest. He buried his face in her neck and teased the sensitive skin there. She tightened around his driving shaft as he picked up the pace.

"Just what I needed," he said.

"Me, too." She gasped.

Digging her fingernails into his shoulders, she came when he thrust faster. Kissing him desperately, she hung on as sweet pleasure released over her in sensuous waves. She wanted to hold on to him, hold on to this for the rest of the night. But she knew they only had a few more precious minutes before Dolly interrupted them. It made the moment sweeter and a little bit naughtier.

She enjoyed every last stroke as he finished with a satisfied groan that was muffled against her mouth. Reba loved kissing him, could kiss him forever. They stumbled back to the bed and kept kissing until Reba heard the Winnebago's door opening.

"Where the hell are you two?" Dolly asked. And then after a few beats: "Are you two having sex?"

"Not anymore," Reba said.

"Oh shit. Sorry. Hang a scarf on the doorknob or something. I'll be back in an hour."

"Make it two," Shane called out.

Reba put her hand over her mouth to keep from giggling.

When the door slammed shut, Shane turned back to

her. "Now, we can take our time."

Reba was all for that and went back to kissing him and rubbing her palms over the hard muscles of his back and shoulders. "Not enough time."

"There's always tomorrow," he murmured against her lips.

All the tomorrows, maybe.

Chapter Fifteen

Shane

Brady, TX
Tuesday before the Odessa Weekend Rodeo

SHANE LOOKED OVER the Brady Cattle Ranch with an eye on how he could improve his own ranch. On the surface, it looked similar, with the vast open pastures, dotted with mesquite trees and native grasses, stretching as far as the eye could see. But the more modern details of the ranch caught his attention. Things that if the UPRC contract worked out, they could put into place at the Viking Ranch.

He and Reba drove up here separately. Shane had been helping Paul Kincaide, the owner of the ranch with the details of settling in his bulls when Reba and Dolly arrived. He watched Dolly charm the old coot and in exchange for a few Instagram lessons, she had full run of the place. Reba had time to give Sverre and the rest of the bulls a thorough examination and was conducting some blood tests to check for allergies or sickness. He was hoping there was some simple explanation over what was causing Sverre to act so erratically.

His brother and Pat were on their way down with Bjorn to replace Sverre on the off chance that Jackson Blevins would come to his senses and pull Sverre from the lineup. Bjorn was a two-year-old bull and wasn't one of their best, but he'd give the cowboys a good ride.

Shane was considering riding out to the pastures to eat with the ranch hands at the chow wagon for dinner when Reba came up to him. She had set up her equipment in one of the empty feed sheds and had gotten to work with her centrifuge. She had been at it for a couple of hours. He didn't want to bother her, but he had been getting a little antsy. So Shane was glad to see her, although the look on her face told him he wasn't going to like what she had to say.

"Can we go somewhere and talk?" she asked softly, her pretty eyes full of sadness and concern.

Oh shit. Shane hoped it wasn't terminal. He loved that stubborn-ass bull. "Here's fine." He patted the porch swing seat next to him. He wished he had taken Paul up on his offer of a pre-dinner beer.

"I don't know how to say this, so I'm going to come right out with it." She held his gaze and he appreciated that. "Sverre has traces of an anabolic steroid in his blood and urine, along with another compound that's too small to trace."

There was a roaring in his ears. What the actual fuck?

"It's not fresh, so it has been in his system for a few days. Based on my tests, and yes, I triple-checked them, he was doped up for Ronnie."

"But they said he was clear." Shane's lips felt numb and

his voice sounded far away to him.

"They lied. Or someone covered it up. This is a huge problem. Someone is tampering with the results. We don't know how many bulls have been affected."

Rage started to edge out the numbness. "Every time you people do these tests, you run the risk of harming my bulls."

"Hey," she said, holding up her hands. "I'm on your side, remember?"

Yeah, he did remember. "Sorry," he muttered and rubbed a hand over his face. "I know it's not you."

"And I know it's not you doing this either. So that leaves us to wonder, who the hell is it?"

"It's got to be your boss Diane who's covering it up. That's why she wanted you out of the trailer." Shane got up and started pacing around.

Reba steadied herself as the swing swerved hard. "Stop jumping to conclusions."

"Is Sverre going to be all right?" he asked.

"Yeah, he's healthy as can be. He could even compete normally in Odessa."

That was a relief, but there were other things to consider. "Can steroids make him sterile?"

"It could, if there was enough of it."

This might not be a bull-riding thing, then. It could be a bull-breeding thing.

Reba went on, "Mainly, you see the steroids being used to make the bull bigger. In this case, with that other substance, I think it might be something that caused him to be more violent and aggressive."

"I'm not going to leave him alone for a moment. Pat, Rick, and I will take shifts. I'll sleep in the damned pen if I have to."

He really needed to beat the hell out of whoever was responsible for this. Except he didn't even know where to begin.

"There's more," Reba said shakily.

Shane wasn't sure he could handle worse news.

"I don't want to. I really don't. But I need to bring this to the UPRC's attention as soon as possible."

Shane whirled on her in disbelief. "They already know. They allowed it to happen and covered it up."

Reba stood up. "We don't know who is involved or why. But I have to report it and get eyes on the whole testing procedure. All of the athletes are at risk, human and animal. We can't just assume that you're the only breeder being targeted."

"What if they don't believe that I'm not involved? What if they try to make my ranch a scapegoat for this? I can't be blacklisted in this industry for something I didn't do. No one will touch us. No one will care if we're innocent or not."

"I'm sorry, Shane," she said. "I'll do my best to keep it discreet."

A bark of a laugh bubbled up from his roiling gut. "There's no way this is going to be kept a secret. If you report this, I'm finished."

This was worse than Abigail leaving him after his wreck. At least he had his family business to fall back on. If word got out that Sverre had been on steroids, he was ruined. Shane had survived no longer being able to ride a bull. How was his family going to survive not being able to breed bulls?

"Reba, please. I need to investigate who is behind this." Shane's thoughts were whirling. "It could be Keith trying to ruin me because of jealousy. Or one of the bull riders because they're pissed that they can't go eight seconds on Sverre. Or another breeder looking to knock out the competition. But anyone who hears that Sverre was tampered with is going to automatically assume we did it to keep him from being rideable. The Viking Ranch can't take that hit to our reputation."

She gripped his upper arm and all he wanted to do was pull her in for a hug. But he couldn't. "Trust me, if there was another way, I'd take it. I…" She turned her back on him. "I have a hard time with whistleblowing. It happened one other time and no one believed me."

"About doping?" He scowled. How prevalent was this shit?

"No," she said. "It was more personal. About Dr. Kilgore."

Shane was momentarily distracted. "What about him?"

Reba's eyes filled with tears. "Now is not the time to get into it."

"Now is exactly the time." And this time he hugged her.

She groaned, but cuddled into him. "Can't this wait?"

"No. Tell me now." For a moment, he didn't think she would.

Then she broke away from his embrace and started to

pace around the small porch. "It was three years ago. After he threw the vase at me?" She looked at him and he nodded to let her know he remembered that she'd told him about the incident. "He immediately tried to make things better. He grabbed me and kissed me."

Shane thought he was angry before. A red haze closed over his vision.

"I reported him to the veterinarian board, but they closed the case. They said it was my word against his. Then Dr. Kilgore said if I pursued it, he would ruin my reputation. And then things got ugly. So I cut and ran. I'm terrified that I'm not going to be believed again." Reba folded her arms over her chest. "I never reported Vidar's injuries because I didn't want to be flagged as a troublemaker in case there wasn't enough proof. That's on me. Maybe if I had, it would have been more difficult to get to Sverre."

"I trusted you to do that." Shane sagged against the porch railing. "It never occurred to me that you wouldn't follow up."

"I'm sorry," she said.

He clasped his palms over his face. What if she was right and filing that report could have stopped Sverre from being drugged? Ronnie died because Sverre had been injected with poison. He couldn't blame Reba for that. She obviously didn't do that. And if someone in her office had been covering up for it, maybe it wouldn't have made a damned bit of difference. But Shane would never know.

"It's going to be all right, Shane. We're going to get to the bottom of this, but we need to let the officials know so someone else doesn't die."

A part of Shane knew that was a reasonable request. Hell, if he was still riding, he would want to know if he had a drug-maddened bull waiting to toss him on his ass. "I just need a few days. Give me until Thursday night before reporting it. I know you're worried about your sister. Sverre will never be alone. No one will have the chance to tamper with him. I don't trust your department with this."

"Do you trust me?"

Did he? Thankfully, she didn't wait for an answer.

"What if it's not just Sverre?" Reba said. "There were too many people who had access to the bulls to assume it's just your ranch."

He closed his eyes. She was right. And yet, he wished she could stand by him and give him the few days. "I'm not asking you to cover this up. I never would do that. All I'm asking for is three days so I can find out who is behind this so my family name doesn't get dragged through the mud. You didn't report Vidar being hurt. Don't report this yet."

"I'm sorry, Shane," she said, her voice breaking. "I can't do that. If we want to catch who is doing this, the UPRC need time to figure out how to stop this. I swear to you, though, that this news won't be released to the public."

"And if Jackson Blevins shit-cans the Viking Ranch anyways? People in this industry talk. The suspicion alone could kill our chances of being a supplier to any other major rodeo. I need you to trust me to handle this."

"I do trust you. I know you didn't drug Sverre. But someone did. Someone could be doing this to other bulls, too. I need to report this and be part of the solution for stopping this from happening again, and clearing your name."

"My name shouldn't have to be cleared," he said.

"I know," she said, rubbing his arm.

They stared at each other. He knew she wasn't going to relent on this. The animals meant too much to her.

"Do what you have to do," he said finally.

"I wish it could be different," she said. "I wish we had the luxury of time."

Shane nodded, disappointment replacing the dread. He wished things were different, too.

"Dolly and I are going to Odessa. We're going to meet with Shelby Miller in the morning and tell her about this."

"Why not with Jackson Blevins? He's the one behind putting LeAnn on Sverre. This should convince him not to."

"Dolly has a rapport with Shelby. She trusts her to do the right thing instead of what will make the company the most money."

It wasn't much hope, but it was something. "All right. I'll see you in Odessa, then."

"Sverre is going to be more dehydrated than usual. Give him some B12 and plenty of water." Reba looked uncomfortable, but then went in for another hug.

Shane didn't want to hug her. Didn't want to hug anyone. He was still too pissed off and the feelings of betrayal reminded him of how he felt when Abigail had left him, even if he knew this situation was entirely different. He patted her awkwardly on the shoulder. "Let me know what Shelby says."

Sniffing, Reba backed up. "I will."

He watched her walk away. A part of him wanted to chase after her and give her a goodbye kiss. But another part of him wondered if it would be a final goodbye if he did. When she was gone, he went in search of Paul. To hell with the pre-dinner beer. Shane needed a pre-dinner whiskey.

Chapter Sixteen

Reba

Odessa, TX

REBA ALTERNATED BETWEEN being pissed off and being depressed. She hated that she couldn't give Shane the time he wanted. But if someone died or an animal was killed, she'd never forgive herself. And yet, what if she did the right thing and told the UPRC everything she knew and they didn't believe her? She'd be doubly fucked. At least if she had given Shane the few days, he wouldn't be hating her right now.

"We can trust Shelby, right?" Reba said as they pulled into the Marriott parking lot where they were meeting her.

"For the tenth time, yes." Dolly checked her makeup in the rearview mirror. Flawless, as always.

"You believe Shane didn't do it, right?"

"Of course," Dolly said, sliding out of the driver's seat. "But someone did. And we need to report it before another bull rider gets hurt. Before LeAnn gets hurt."

The thought of LeAnn getting on a tampered bull made Reba want to bite her nails down to the quick. How Dylan could watch her ride after everything he had been through was beyond her.

"What if they already know about this and don't care?" LeAnn said. "What if they think we're troublemakers?"

"They better not know, because we will be troublemakers. I can guaran-damn-tee you that."

She needed to be fearless like Dolly, but Reba's knees were shaking and she felt like she was on the verge of tears. She wanted to talk to Shane. She wanted to run the hell out of here and give him the few days he asked for. She owed him her loyalty more than she did this organization. But it wasn't about her right now. It was about the safety of all the athletes and Reba needed to put on her big-girl panties and suck it up.

They walked through the lobby and got directions to the boardroom where the UPRC had set up a meeting area for pre-rodeo business.

Reba stopped Dolly from opening the door to the suite. "She needs to be discreet. Shane's livelihood is at stake. And LeAnn's life is at risk."

"Shelby will handle it," Dolly said. "She'll get to the bottom of this."

"I hope you're right," Reba muttered.

Dolly pushed open the door and walked into the room. But then she stopped dead and Reba nearly bumped into her.

"What are you doing here?" Dolly asked.

Reba peered around her shoulder and saw Nash Weaver talking with Shelby.

"Close the door and lock it," Shelby said.

That didn't sound ominous at all.

Reba locked the door as Dolly moved into the room.

"Nash is my brother," Shelby said. "He also used to be a federal agent."

"What?" Dolly stopped in her tracks.

Reba crossed her arms over her chest. "We didn't do anything wrong." This was utter bullshit.

"It's not you two I'm worried about. I don't have anything solid, but I think Jackson Blevins is doing some illegal things. Nash recently took an early retirement from the bureau, and he's helping me out."

"You're undercover?" Dolly said. "Of course. That's why I couldn't find a damned thing about your past. And why you're such a shitty bull rider."

"Hey," Nash said. "I'm not that bad."

"Yes, you are," Shelby and Dolly said together.

If Shane's family's future wasn't on the line this might actually be amusing. "So that's why you were in the restricted area," Reba said. "What were you looking for?"

Nash gave her that smile again but didn't answer her.

"Have a seat," Shelby said. "Based on what Dolly hinted at in her phone call, I wanted Nash to hear this, too."

Great, now her palms were sweating. She and Dolly sat down at the conference room table. "What exactly did Dolly tell you?" Reba asked, side-eyeing her sister.

"She said that LeAnn was in danger, and you had proof."

"And you think Jackson Blevins is trying to harm her?" Reba asked.

"Why don't you tell us what you came here to say?" Nash said.

"Why don't you back off my sister?" Dolly snapped.

"It's okay." Reba put a restraining hand on Dolly's arm. "We went to see Sverre. Dolly because she needed some footage for promo, and me because Shane Calland asked me to give his bull an exam to see why he was acting out."

Shelby leaned forward. "And what did you find?"

"I examined his blood and urine samples and there were traces of an undetermined substance along with anabolic steroids."

"What type of substance?" Nash asked.

"What do you think undetermined means?" Dolly asked.

"Dolly, please. I don't know. What I do know is that the Viking Ranch was not behind this."

"How do you know this?" Shelby asked.

"I've been to their ranch, and I've seen no sign of tampering. I also know that Shane is violently opposed to it."

"I need a sample of the blood and urine. I can get access to more sophisticated equipment that might be able to narrow down that substance," Nash said.

"I have samples in my RV under refrigeration. I can bring those to you." Reba started to get up.

"When we're done here," Shelby said. "Why did Sverre's original tests come back clean?"

"I don't know if they did," Reba said. "I wasn't allowed to complete any of them."

"You weren't?" Nash exchanged a look with his sister. "What would you have done if you found evidence that Sverre had been injected with a foreign substance?"

"The same thing that happened yesterday," Reba said,

trying to keep a grip on her temper. "I would have reported it." Of course, she would have told Dolly first and freaked out about the decision.

"And Diane knew that?" Shelby asked.

Reba scoffed. "Actually, she thought I'd cover for Shane. That's why she pulled me off the testing. Dr. Victor Lance did the tests."

"Are you sure?" Nash asked.

"He was working on them when I left," Reba said. "Whether he concluded them, I don't know."

"Who else could have analyzed the samples?" Nash asked.

Reba was beginning to feel cross-examined. "Me, Victor, or Diane."

"So, either Diane or Victor are in on this," Shelby said. "Otherwise, we would have received the positive test back before now. I'm calling in an independent lab to do the tests for this weekend."

"I think that's a good idea," Reba said. "And I think that you need to call off the exhibition with LeAnn on Sverre."

"I can't completely do that," Shelby said. "We sold tickets based on Sverre and we need to give the audience a show that they'll appreciate."

"Not at the risk of my baby sister," Reba said.

"Who is another top athlete that you can't afford to risk on a bull that you know has been shot up with a substance," Dolly said.

"Although," Reba said reluctantly, "it will be out of his system by the time the rodeo starts."

"Whose side are you on?" Dolly said, exasperated.

"Look," Shelby said, "I'm going to modify Jackson's ad campaign that he wanted you to do. Instead of Killer on a killer, I want you to do a comeback story with a twist."

"What type of twist?" Dolly asked.

"I spoke to Shane Calland this morning. He's agreed to ride Sverre."

"Shane can't ride a bull," Reba said, feeling like she heard wrong. "His leg is messed up."

"He was actually eager to do it. I think he plans on beating his own bull's undefeatable streak."

Reba shook her head. "It's not safe."

"This will work out for us in several ways," Shelby said. "It will satisfy Jackson's need to cash in on Sverre's notoriety. It will satisfy our fans' need for drama. They get to see a rodeo hero come back from retirement and the stakes are either he will beat his own bull's record or Sverre will continue to be undefeated. Shane gets to assuage any rumors about tampering by agreeing to ride Sverre. If he didn't think he was safe, he wouldn't risk his life. And it gives us time to protect our athletes, both human and animal, while we investigate if any others have been drugged."

"But we know Sverre was tampered with," Reba said. "And we don't know how many others have been. The only safe thing to do is skip the bull-riding event for Odessa until we can get your independent lab results back."

But Shelby was already shaking her head. "I can't do that. The fans bought their tickets based on the bull-riding events. We can't disappoint them."

"She's right," Dolly said.

Reba glared at her sister. She hadn't wanted to trade LeAnn's safety for Shane's.

"Besides," Nash said, "I'll be more focused on your boss Diane and Dr. Victor for this rodeo. If they are covering up for the doping, we can nail them if their findings don't match what the independent lab come up with. In the meantime, I'll see if I can find out who is injecting the bulls," Nash said. "And then see if they know how Jackson is involved."

"Shane's agreed to give Nash access to his area and not to add any additional security," Shelby said.

"What makes you so sure Jackson Blevins is behind all this?" Reba asked.

"He's been making some decisions around here that are not in the best interest of the rodeo," Shelby said. "If I had known some of the things he had been planning, I wouldn't have merged the two organizations. If we can't make up some of the money that we've lost and if I can't stop the egregious spending and bad policies, the UPRC could go under."

"You may want to reconsider only having three exclusive breeders providing the stock supply then," Reba muttered.

"Wait," Shelby said. "What are you talking about?"

Reba stared at her. How could she not know about this? "Shane was offered one of three exclusive contracts to be the UPRC's sole stock supplier for bulls for the next five years."

Shelby was already shaking her head. "That's not something we've discussed or agreed on."

"I'm not lying." Reba stood up in anger.

Shelby looked puzzled. "I believe you."

Shock replaced anger and Reba sat down. "You do?"

"Yes."

"About everything?"

"Yes."

Reba took in a shaky breath. "Just like that?"

"Just like that," Shelby said and the kindness in her voice had tears pricking at the corners of Reba's eyes.

"As far as I know, Shane's already signed the contract though," Reba said.

Nash and Shelby exchanged another one of their grim looks. "Who are the other two breeders?" Nash asked.

"I don't know," Reba said. "Shane was asked to keep it quiet until they announced it."

"Thank you," Shelby said. "I'll look into it. And thank you for being so open and honest. It couldn't have been easy to report your boyfriend's bull."

It hadn't been, but not because Reba didn't want to be open and honest.

"We need you to keep quiet about the false reports so you don't tip our hand and spook the bad guys," Nash said.

It was working out just how Shane wanted it. The doping report would be kept under wraps, and the UPRC would be actively searching out who did this.

"I can help with the testing."

Shelby shook her head. "Not this time. We don't want them to know about the independent lab either until it's too late for them to do anything about it. Just do whatever

Diane tells you to do. You can keep an eye out on Victor if you're discreet."

"I can do that." What she really wanted to do was keep Shane off that bull, off any bull really.

"Because of the nature of Nash's involvement, we're not going to be able to keep you informed. Please keep this meeting and Nash's purpose a secret. If Jackson is involved in something more serious than trying to make the rodeo more exciting—" Shelby used finger quotes to offset the last word. "I want to make sure we can obtain solid evidence before going to the authorities."

"We can keep our mouths shut," Dolly said.

Nash snorted, which earned him a death glare from Dolly.

"When Jackson has a shit-fit about it being Shane instead of LeAnn on that bull, I'll make sure he knows it was me who overrode his decision. You shouldn't see any fallout from it, but if you do, let me know immediately, and I'll put a stop to it," Shelby said to Dolly.

"Thanks," Dolly said.

As they got up to leave, Reba decided to put all her cards on the table. "One other thing," she said.

Shelby raised her eyebrow. "I'm almost afraid to hear this."

Almost as much as I'm afraid to tell you.

"There's a new bull breeder who may be looking to work with the UPRC. His name is Chuck Kilgore."

Shelby frowned and then clicked a few keys on her laptop. "Yes. I see his application right here."

Reba froze. Her boyfriend was a rival breeder. No one

in their right mind would believe her. They would think she was trying to hurt Shane's competition. No, that was Dr. Kilgore still renting space in her head. It didn't matter if they didn't believe her. It was past time that she told her truth. And she would keep telling her truth until someone believed her. "I used to work for him. He's got anger management issues and his office was toxic. He got violent and would throw things. He…" Reba swallowed and looked at Dolly. Dolly reached over and gave her hand a squeeze. "He threw a vase that shattered against the wall. It cut my face. While I was still recovering from the shock, he grabbed my shoulders and kissed me."

"He fucking did what?" Dolly shouted.

"He had always been handsy, giving unwanted shoulder massages and shit like that. I think when he kissed me, he was trying to control me rather than anything sexual, but…" Reba shrugged. "I don't know."

"Did you press charges?" Nash growled.

"I reported him to the veterinarian bureau. They didn't believe me and closed the case against him. He threatened to ruin my life if I pursued it. So I didn't. I'm bringing this up now because if you do hire him as one of your breeders, make sure he isn't alone with any women workers. And I wanted you to have a heads-up about his behavior."

"Thank you," Shelby said. "For what it's worth, I believe you. And I will be very careful in my dealings with him."

This time, a few tears slipped out. Reba didn't call attention to them by swiping them away. But she didn't trust her voice either. So she just nodded.

Dolly didn't let go of her hand until they were back by the RV. Nash had followed them out to get the samples. While Reba was getting them from inside, she heard Dolly ask Nash, "I don't suppose you can give me advice on how to set up a sting operation to nail that asshole's pecker to a wall?"

"Are we talking figuratively or literally?" Nash asked.

Reba came out carrying the samples in a cooler. She saw Dolly shrug one shoulder. "Whichever."

Chapter Seventeen

Shane

Odessa, TX—UPRC All-Star Rodeo

SHANE HAD NO problem with getting back into the bull-riding routine. He was having a hard time ditching Reba's phone calls. The excuse he told himself was that he was just too tired after training for the past few days on the Brady farm to speak to her, but he knew he was being a chickenshit. He wasn't ghosting her. He just didn't know what to say to her. And whatever was said, he didn't want to do it over the phone.

So, once he got to the rodeo grounds, Shane went looking for her. She wasn't in the veterinarian trailer, but one of the vet techs said she was in horse barn A, so he made his way there. When he got there, he saw Reba all right. She was talking with Abigail.

It almost made him want to turn on his heel and run back to the bullpens. But he had been a coward for the last few days. It was time for him to man up and have some tough conversations with Reba. He just hoped his ex-wife wasn't giving her advice on how to dump his sorry ass.

But as he got closer, he overheard them talking about

Starshine, Ronnie's horse.

"I just want to know that Starshine is going to a good home," Abigail said.

"Dylan Porter may just be starting up his horse rescue farm, but he knows what he's doing."

"I know that he's married to your sister," Abigail retorted. "And you wouldn't say a bad word about him. Vanessa should have sold Starshine to me." She patted the horse's neck.

"Well, she didn't. And be glad of it because the renal feed and care Starshine needs is going to take a lot of time and expense."

"Are you saying I would let a horse suffer?"

Shane could tell that Abigail was itching for a fight.

"No, I'm saying Starshine is Dylan Porter's horse. And he will take care of her very well."

"I know Lou Porter," Shane said, coming up to them. "Dylan's rescue is on his property. They're good people."

Abigail glared at him for interrupting.

"What do you want?" Reba crossed her arms and matched Abigail glare for glare.

"I wanted to talk to you."

"I'm working," she snapped.

He couldn't blame her for being mad at him. "I wanted a few words before I got on Sverre today."

Abigail slugged him in the arm. "You're an asshole for doing that."

Reba nodded.

Great, they were ganging up on him. Guess he had his answer.

"Whatever." He turned and walked out of the barn.

Reba caught up to him a few minutes later on the golf cart. "Get in."

He sat down next to her and she peeled off away from the barns. She didn't say a word to him until they were by her RV. "I need to talk to you in private," she said.

At least they wouldn't have an audience for this. He braced himself for the big goodbye when the door behind him closed and they were inside. He staggered back when she threw herself into his arms.

"Why are you doing this?" she asked, hugging him tight.

Okay, they were going to get the bull-riding thing out of the way first. "It's a win-win situation."

"Not if you get injured."

"I've been practicing," he said defensively. "I'm not going into this cold."

"On Sverre?" she said, pushing him back.

"No. I'm saving him for today."

She squinted at him. "How's your leg? Your ankle?"

"They're not too happy with me."

"How about your brain?" she asked. "Your heart?"

His heart ached worse than his leg. "My brain thinks this is a good idea. It's only eight seconds."

"I'm so worried about you," she said. "Why didn't you call me?"

Shane sighed and sat down. "I wanted to put off the inevitable as long as possible."

"What are you talking about?" she asked.

She was so pretty, it made his heart hurt to look at her.

He couldn't help himself and had to rub his knuckles across her cheek. Reba surprised him by sitting in his lap and cupping his face in her hands. "Don't do this," she said.

"It's too late now to back out."

"No, it's not," she said.

"I'm doing this, Reba." He pressed his forehead against hers. "I understand if you no longer want to be with me. Chances are the Viking Ranch is going to lose this contract and I'll be a broken-down ex bull rider again without any prospects."

"I'm more worried about you," she said. "One bad fall and you could be in a wheelchair, or worse."

"The bullfighters will have my back. I know how to land. And Sverre knows me. It'll be okay."

"You don't know that," she said.

"I do," he said, giving in to temptation and rubbing her back.

"Shelby believed me," Reba said. "She's keeping this all quiet while she conducts her own investigation. She might know who is behind this."

That was news to him. "Who?"

She tilted her head back. "Maybe if you called me back this week, you'd already know."

His lips twitched in a smile. "I didn't want you to break up with me over the phone."

"Why would I break up with you? I may not like you riding Sverre, but I still care about you. Hell, I probably love you." She looked a little shocked at the admission.

"Don't play with my emotions," he said gruffly.

"I'm not," she said and tried to scoot off his lap.

He wouldn't let her. "I care about you, too. Hell, I probably love you, as well. No, there's no probably about it. I love you, Reba Keller."

"Good, because I'm not going anywhere. If you're determined to ride that stupid bull, at least he won't be doped up."

"We hope," Shane said darkly. He had agreed to be lax in security and he hoped his bull didn't suffer for it.

"Shelby has an undercover agent working in the bull-pens." She leaned in and whispered in his ear. "It's Nash Weaver. He's trying to catch the person drugging the bulls in the act. Or at least gather more evidence. If someone goes to inject Sverre, he'll stop it."

"I hope you're right."

"I'm worried Sverre is going to throw you."

"He probably will," Shane admitted.

"Then why are you doing this?" She smacked his shoulders in exasperation.

"To prove that the bull isn't a killer."

"And if he is?" Reba nibbled on her lip.

"He's not. I raised that bull. He's going to buck and jump and whirl. But he's not going to go after me once I'm on the ground. And if he does," Shane hurried to say when she took a deep breath to say something. "Barney and Taylor and the rest of the boys will be right there to get me to safety."

"I hate this," she said, her eyes filling with tears.

"I'll survive this. I can survive anything as long as I know you're going to be there after the ride."

"I'll be there," she said. "You can count on it." Her phone buzzed. She glared at it. "Shit, I've got to get back to work. Are we good?"

"We're good," he said.

"Call me back next time instead of having me eat voicemail?"

"I promise," he said. Shane still held her close as she slid off his lap. "You really don't want to dump me even if the ranch loses the UPRC contract?"

"Of course not," she said. "You'll bounce back from it and even if you don't, it doesn't matter to me. And based on Shelby's Miller's reaction about only having three breeders for the UPRC, I'm not sure that's going to even be an issue anymore."

"What do you mean?" he asked, frowning. "I signed a contract."

Reba held up her hands. "I'm not a lawyer, and I don't know how the UPRC is set up. All I'm saying is Shelby hadn't known about the contract. But be that as it may, it doesn't matter if you are in the UPRC or not. I want to be with you, Shane Calland. I don't care if you're a rancher, a bull rider, or a janitor. I just want you."

"I want you, too," he said hoarsely.

"Well, too damned bad because I've got a cow about to give birth." She gave him a hard kiss on the mouth. "But if you can still walk after the rodeo, I'm all yours."

"Now that's the incentive I need to stay healthy," he said.

SHANE WALKED AMONG the other bull riders, trying to regain the feeling that he had when he had been in active competition. Was the thrill of hearing the crowd cheer for him still there? Yeah, but it was muted. He found himself looking for Reba's face in the crowd. He never did that when he was married to Abigail or with anyone else that he had been dating.

"Did you hear about the big hullaballoo?" Barney asked.

"I'm sure you're going to tell me." Shane watched as Pat and Tommy walked Sverre into the gate area. He snorted and slammed himself into the rails, making some of the cowboys jump away.

"That other veterinarian, Dr. Lance? He got escorted out of the rodeo by a couple tough-looking cops."

"Oh yeah?" Shane said. "Did they say why?"

"No one knows a fucking thing," Barney said. "But the rumor is he's been up to no good around the bulls and some of the broncs."

"Really?" Shane said.

"You think he stuck Sverre?" Barney said.

"I hope not."

"Just be careful."

"Always am." Shane heard the announcer call his name and the crowd was getting antsy. He turned and looked for Reba, but he didn't see her. He'd go search her out when all this was over and kiss her senseless.

Unless he was senseless.

As he moved to get settled on the bull, he caught Nash Weaver's eyes. Nash gave him the thumbs-up signal. Shane took that to mean that this ride was going to be all up to him and Sverre.

Sverre bucked and snorted when he settled on top of him. He was raring to go as Shane got his ropes in order and then, before he could have any second thoughts, the gate was open and they were on their way.

Reba

REBA NEVER THOUGHT of herself as a clinger, but she hung on to LeAnn for all six seconds of Shane's ride. Shane put up a good fight, but in the end, Sverre was not going to let him go for eight seconds. He shook Shane up and down and finally with a last buck, Shane was tossed off.

Sverre kicked up his back legs and shook his head, but Shane was clear and limping toward the rails. Marty Kreeger was there with a lasso around Sverre's neck and without any more drama, Sverre was hustled back to the pens.

"I could have ridden him for the eight seconds," LeAnn said.

"Maybe you'll get your chance." Reba didn't want to let go of her sister, but she did. "Just be damned careful."

"You sound like Mom." LeAnn rolled her eyes.

Reba hurried back to the bullpen area where Shane was getting good-naturedly teased about his ride.

"Knew you didn't have it in you anymore," Keith said, with his arm around Abigail.

Maybe not so good-naturedly.

"He's a tough bull," Nash said.

"They're all tough to you," one of the other bull riders teased.

"Reba…" A hand on her arm stopped her from running to Shane and throwing her arms around him.

"What?" she said, annoyed when she turned and saw it was Dr. Kilgore who held her. "Get your hands off me!" Out of the corner of her eye, she saw Shane and Nash look in her direction.

"Easy there, sweetheart." Kilgore raised his hands and gave her a fake smile that didn't reach his eyes.

She remembered the warning look he used to give all of them. "I'm not your sweetheart," she said. "And you don't belong back here."

"Hey," Keith said. "He's with me."

She ignored him.

"There's no need to be rude," Kilgore said between his teeth. "I've been trying to reach you about a job offer."

"I have a job," Reba said. Even if she wasn't too happy with Diane and the UPRC right now, it was miles better than what she'd had.

"I can offer you much better. I've heard about your troubles." Kilgore looked over her shoulder and took a step back. Reba imagined that Shane was bearing down on them. "I can pay you a lot more than what you're making now and you'd have full run of all my animals. You'd be in charge of all testing and decisions. We need you back on the team."

"I wouldn't work for a dickhead like you at twice the

salary. You have the temper of a doped-up bull, the manners of a bull rider on a bender, and…" She took a deep breath. "You're an evil fuck." Reba was shaking, but damn, it felt good to say all that.

"How dare you," he sputtered.

"How dare I?" she asked. "You really want me to explain how I dare with my boyfriend and family so close by."

"You're hysterical," he said and backed away from her.

She risked a glance over her shoulder and saw not only Shane and Nash, but also Dylan, Dolly, and LeAnn almost literally at her back.

"And you are no longer worth my time." Reba dismissed Kilgore with a look and then jumped into Shane's arms. "Congratulations," she said.

"You, too." He kissed her.

Oblivious to the crowd around them, she wrapped her legs around his waist and let him carry her off to somewhere more private.

Epilogue

Reba

Six months later…
Charlo, MT—the Viking Ranch

REBA WAS LOOKING through bridal magazines with Lainey and Shane's mother, Mary, while Shane and Rick were getting Ragnar into the trailer for his next big date.

"Don't worry, I'm not going to make you wear this." Lainey flashed a picture of a truly ugly bridesmaid dress.

"Good," Reba said. "Because I'd hate to get called away on an emergency on your wedding day."

"We could have a double wedding," Mary said. She had stopped dropping subtle hints a few months ago.

"No," Reba said. "Lainey and Rick deserve their own day."

"It's just that Bill and I will be moving to Florida, and it'll be difficult to come back here for a while."

"You'll be back once the weather sticks at a hundred degrees for a few months," Shane said, coming up on the porch. He leaned down to give Reba a thorough kiss.

"I don't think it gets that hot on the water," Mary said.

"Don't worry. We'll give you plenty of notice when we decide to get married," Reba said. She exchanged an amused look with Shane. They had already decided on a date next year, but they didn't want to steal the attention away from Lainey and Rick's wedding. They were going to wait until after the new couple was back from their honeymoon before making an official announcement. Dolly had already figured it out, but swore she wouldn't say a word.

"Come in the kitchen with me," Shane said, taking her hand and lifting her up from her seat.

"He can make his own damned sandwich," Mary called after them.

"I don't think that's what he's looking for," Lainey said dryly.

In the kitchen, they were alone and took the opportunity to share more sweet kisses. When the front door banged, they sprang apart, and Reba made a show of opening the refrigerator door and was rummaging through it by the time Shane's father came in.

"Can I make you a sandwich, Bill?" Reba asked.

"I wouldn't say no to a roast beef and onion one."

"You got it." She made them all one, minus the onion for her and Shane in case there was more kissing in the near future.

She and Shane took their sandwiches into the living room and sat on the couch. "Dolly called me today," she said. "She wanted me to know that Victor Lance finally confessed to doping up Sverre. The UPRC fired him and they're pressing charges. They have the evidence on him, dead to rights. He's claiming that he acted alone. My boss,

Diane, wasn't involved at all apparently."

"What about Jackson Blevins?"

"He skated clean, too, but Dolly thinks there's something else going on. Nash is going to stick around for another season. Dolly is losing her mind because she has to create a buzz around him and, well, he still sucks. LeAnn suggested that he head over to Trent Campbell's school at the Three Sisters Ranch in Last Stand, Texas during the off-season."

"It couldn't hurt," Shane said. "Did Victor Lance say why he drugged my bull? Was it just my bull?"

"Yeah, it was just Sverre. He said he was placing bets on the outcome."

"I'll have to talk to a few lawyers and see if we can sue the pants off him," Shane said, after chewing thoughtfully a few times.

"That's a far cry from wanting to kill someone for whipping your bull," Reba said.

"Did he do that, too?"

"Not that he said, but I wouldn't put it past him."

"Speaking of shitty people and the things that they do, has Dolly told you about Dr. Kilgore yet?" Shane asked.

Reba cocked her head at him. "No, what did that asshole do now?"

Shane rubbed his hands together in glee. "I can't believe I know something before Dolly."

"Don't get used to it," she said dryly.

"Lou Porter told me that not only will the Kilgore Ranch not be a supplier to the UPRC, but a certain veterinarian lost his license."

"Are you teasing me?" Reba said, shock and joy warring with her. "It's not April Fools' Day is it?"

"Nope. It seems when Shelby Miller did a little digging, she found that one of his current vet techs, Penny Markson, has also filed a complaint against him. Penny was on the verge of withdrawing it when Shelby told her in confidence that it wasn't Dr. Kilgore's first time."

"I know Penny," Reba said. "Well, not really. I talked to her awhile back. She gave me a coupon for Starshine's feed for Ronnie. It never occurred to me that he was still doing that shit. I suppose it should have."

"Well, now that Penny is standing firm on her complaint, three other women came forward. He's history."

Reba closed her eyes as tears threatened. Chuck Kilgore would never practice again and, hopefully, he'd never be able to hurt any other women again. At any rate, the world now knew him for the shit-heel he was. Vindication should have felt sweet, but while she was relieved, she was sad it had gone on as long as it did.

"That's great news," she said, holding his hand tightly.

"Did Diane mention hiring anyone to replace Victor?"

"The last time I talked to her was at the final rodeo of the season. I'm sure she'll have someone by the time the UPRC starts up again."

"At least, you'll get your job responsibilities back," Shane said.

"It'll do until after the wedding," she said. "Then I think I'll stay here and help you out on the farm."

"Really?" Shane asked with a big grin.

"Really?" Bill said from the doorway in the kitchen.

Shane shook his head. "When are you moving to Florida again?" he asked his father.

"Not soon enough," Bill replied and popped back into the kitchen.

"You got that right," Shane muttered and slung his arm around her. "Are you sure you won't miss traveling from rodeo to rodeo?"

"I'll get that fix by riding with you when you go," she said. "Are you sure that you're done with bull riding?"

"More than done with it," he said. "All I want now is to build a new life with you and bull riding isn't a part of that."

"What about kittens?" she asked, sneaking a look over her shoulder at Bill who was still eavesdropping.

"No more kittens," Bill said.

Shane leaned in to kiss her. "All the kittens you want."

"I love you," Reba said.

"I love you, too."

The End

If you enjoyed *The Cowboy's Untamed Heart*,
check out the other books in the

Sweethearts of the Rodeo series

Book 1: *The Cowboy's Prize*

Book 2: *The Cowboy's Untamed Heart*

Book 3: *The Undercover Cowboy*

Available now at your favorite online retailer!

More books by Jamie K. Schmidt

Three Sisters Ranch series

Book 1: *The Cowboy's Daughter*

Book 2: *The Cowboy's Hunt*

Book 3: *The Cowboy's Heart*

Book 4: *A Cowboy for April*

Book 5: *A Cowboy for June*

Book 6: *A Cowboy for Merry*

Other Title

A Spark of Romance

Available now at your favorite online retailer!

About the Author

USA Today bestselling author, Jamie K. Schmidt, writes erotic contemporary love stories and paranormal romances. Her steamy, romantic comedy, Life's a Beach, reached #65 on USA Today, #2 on Barnes & Noble and #9 on Amazon and iBooks. Her Club Inferno series from Random House's Loveswept line has hit both the Amazon and Barnes & Noble top one hundred lists. The first book in the series, Heat, put her on the USA Today bestseller list for the first time, and is a #1 Amazon bestseller. Her book Stud is a 2018 Romance Writers of America Rita® Finalist in Erotica. Her dragon paranormal romance series has been called "fun and quirky" and "endearing." Partnered with New York Times bestselling author and former porn actress, Jenna Jameson, Jamie's hardcover debut, SPICE, continues Jenna's FATE trilogy.

Thank you for reading

The Cowboy's Untamed Heart

If you enjoyed this book, you can find more from all our great authors at TulePublishing.com, or from your favorite online retailer.

TULE
PUBLISHING

Printed in Great Britain
by Amazon

42866001R00138